CALMER WATERS

Where New Beginnings and Unexpected Love Sail Together

Book Two of the Navigating New Beginnings Series

REBECCA ROBERTS

Published by Hemingway Publishers

Cover design by Hemingway Publishers

ISBN: Printed in the United States

Dedication

To all women who have stepped bravely into life's transitions, through retirement, loss, reinvention, or the quiet unfolding of a new chapter, this book is for you.

To your courage in facing the unknown, your grace in letting go, and your wisdom in embracing what truly matters. To the lives you have lived with passion, the challenges you have overcome, and the dreams that still call you forward.

May you honor your past, celebrate your present, and step into your future with confidence, joy, and the unshakable knowing that the best is yet to come.

Rebecca

Contents

Dedication iii

Chapter 1 1

Chapter 2 12

Chapter 3 23

Chapter 4 34

Chapter 5 44

Chapter 6 54

Chapter 7 64

Chapter 8 75

Chapter 9 85

Chapter 10 96

Chapter 11 106

Chapter 12 117

Chapter 13 126

Chapter 14 135

Chapter 15 145

Chapter 16 155

Chapter 17 166

Chapter 18 176

Chapter 19 186

Chapter 20 194

Chapter 21 204

Chapter 21 213

Chapter 22 222

Chapter 23 231

Chapter 24 242

Author's Note..262

Chapter 1

The morning air carried the scent of salt and fresh bread as Tessa, Julia, and Seren, friends for nearly forty years, wound their way through Valletta's honey-colored streets. Limestone buildings rose around them, their weathered facades telling stories of centuries past. Wrought iron balconies burst with crimson bougainvillea, creating splashes of color against the ancient stone.

"This is exactly what I needed," Tessa trailed her fingers along a sun-warmed wall.

Her silver bob gleamed in the Mediterranean light, immaculate as always despite the gentle breeze. "No more legal briefs, no more client crises, no more…" She paused, her voice dropping. "Philandering husbands."

Julia linked arms with her friend. "No more putting yourself last," she agreed, hazel eyes warm with understanding. "Forty years is enough of that."

"Well, I for one am thrilled to be here celebrating with you," Seren declared, her enthusiasm drawing glances from passing locals. She wore a flowing bohemian graphic maxi skirt beneath a billowy white blouse that fluttered dramatically as she gestured toward the harbor spread below them. "The universe has aligned to bring us here, together, at this perfect moment in our lives."

They climbed stone steps between centuries-old buildings, emerging onto a terrace where a small café overlooked the Grand Harbor. Below them, their cruise ship, the polished white Aurelia, waited at the dock like a promise.

"Look at her," Julia murmured as they settled at a table beneath a striped awning. "Eleven days aboard that beauty."

"Eleven days to celebrate happy endings and new beginnings," Tessa added, studying the menu.

Julia exaggerated a look around, "You don't see Avery or Daniel Price anywhere around, do you?"

They chuckled in unison at the reminder of their last cruise, a Cyntera corporate retreat full of corporate intrigue and family secrets.

Their waiter appeared, describing local specialties with pride. They ordered rabbit stew, Lampuki pie, and a carafe of crisp local wine, then fell into comfortable silence as they watched boats crisscross the harbor.

"I still can't believe you let James buy you out of the house," Julia said finally, turning to Tessa. "James must have been shocked."

Tessa's lips curved into a satisfied smile. "His divorce lawyer called mine three times to confirm I wasn't contesting the settlement terms. Apparently, walking away from the money fight wasn't what he expected."

"Men like James only understand value in dollar signs," Seren pronounced, pouring wine for each of them. "But freedom… that's priceless."

Their food arrived, fragrant and steaming. As they ate, the conversation flowed as easily as it had since their twenties, when three ambitious young women found kindred spirits in one another.

"So," Tessa dabbed her lips with a napkin, "Julia's living her second-chance romance with the dashing Marine, I'm officially untethered from forty years of marital fiction, and Seren," She cocked her head.

"What's this about selling Marwood Travels? You built that business from nothing."

Seren's eyes sparkled. "I've loved every moment: planning travel and adventures for others. But now, I feel called to do something else."

"The life wellness and spiritual retreats?" Julia asked.

"Exactly." Seren leaned forward, suddenly serious. "I've been testing the waters with weekend workshops, but I want to create something transformational. I've been considering opening my own retreat center. Someplace women can come to find clarity after major life events and transition."

"Like us," Tessa observed quietly.

"Precisely like us." Seren raised her glass. "Three sixty-something women, reinventing themselves. If that's not worth celebrating, what is?"

They clinked glasses, the sound bright in the clear air.

"Speaking of reinvention," Tessa's tone turned teasing, "how does it feel to be living with Reid after all these years? Forty years is quite the delayed gratification."

A soft flush colored Julia's cheeks. "It feels… right, like time folded back on itself. We wake up every morning and watch the sun rise over the Chesapeake Bay. Sometimes I can't believe it's real."

"You deserve every moment of it," Tessa said, squeezing her friend's hand. "Both of you do."

Seren's attention had drifted to the harbor, where crew members were visible on the Aurelia's deck. "Eleven days at sea," she mused. "Eleven days of new possibilities."

Tessa followed her gaze. "New possibilities," she echoed, her voice carrying a note of hesitation. "I must admit, I'm at a loss right now for possibilities."

"Oh, darling." Seren's laugh rang out. "The universe gives us what we need when we need it."

Julia raised an eyebrow. "And what do we need, O wise one?"

"Adventure," Seren declared. "Challenge. Perhaps even…" she wiggled her eyebrows dramatically "romance."

* * *

Captain Delgado stood on the main deck of the Aurelia, his silver hair catching the Mediterranean sunlight as he conferred with his Chief of Security. His weathered face remained impassive, but tension lined his shoulders beneath the crisp white uniform.

"The manifest shows three more VIPs arriving within the hour," the CSO reported, scrolling through his tablet.

The captain's piercing blue eyes suddenly shifted focus, drawn to the gangway where three elegant women were boarding. His heart gave an unexpected lurch when he recognized the sleek silver bob and poised figure of Tessa Monroe. Beside her walked two companions, one with chestnut hair and thoughtful eyes, the other with bohemian flair and animated gestures.

"Tessa," he murmured, a smile warming his features.

The CSO followed his gaze. "Someone you know, Captain?"

"Si, from an Iridessa voyage." Manny straightened his already-immaculate jacket.

"A friend."

A welcome sight amid the complications of this unusual assignment. The Aurelia wasn't his regular vessel, and this voyage carried undercurrents that had nothing to do with the azure Mediterranean waters. Having a familiar face aboard, especially one who had brought such warmth to a previous cruise, felt like an unexpected gift.

"The gentlemen boarded earlier and have settled in their staterooms," the CSO continued. "Security protocols are in place as requested. We've deployed plainclothes personnel in the public areas."

Manny nodded, only half-listening as he watched Tessa laugh at something her bohemian friend said. She looked different somehow: lighter, more vibrant than he remembered.

"And our special guest?"

"No sign yet. We'll alert you the moment they arrive."

"Grazie. Keep me informed of any developments." Manny clasped the officer's shoulder. "If you need me, I'll be welcoming our guests."

He moved with purpose across the deck, his tall figure commanding respect from passing crew members who snapped to attention. But as he approached Tessa and her friends, his captain's persona softened into something more genuine.

* * *

The grand atrium of the Aurelia shimmered with golden light as Tessa, Julia, and Seren made their way across the polished marble floor. Above them, the spectacular Aurum Spiral, a swirling sculptural installation of amber glass and gold leaf, caught the afternoon sun streaming through floor-to-ceiling windows.

"Our suites are on Deck 8," Seren consulted her phone. "The Panorama Suites, with balconies facing port side."

"Lead the way," Tessa adjusted her shoulder bag, glancing around at the elegant space. "I'm ready for a long soak in that marble tub they promised."

They wove between clusters of arriving passengers toward the bank of elevators when a deep, rich voice rolled across the atrium.

Captain Manuel Delgado crossed the atrium floor with the easy confidence of a man completely at home on his vessel. His silver hair caught the light, and his crisp white uniform set off his sun-bronzed skin. His blue eyes crinkled at the corners as his smile spread wide.

"Signora Monroe," he called, his Italian accent rich with pleasure. "What a wonderful surprise to see you again."

Tessa turned, recognition and delight flooding her face. "Captain Delgado! I had no idea you'd be commanding the Aurelia."

"A temporary arrangement," he explained. "But now, a most fortunate one."

"I couldn't believe it," he continued, "when I saw you come aboard. I thought my eyes were playing a cruel trick." He reached her, placing his hands on her shoulders and leaning in to press a kiss to first one cheek, then the other.

Heat bloomed from where his lips brushed her skin, radiating outward and downward in a rush that left her momentarily speechless. His subtle cologne, notes of cedar and sea salt, wrapped around her senses.

"What are you doing on the Aurelia?" Tessa finally managed, aware that Julia and Seren had fallen conspicuously silent beside her. "I thought the Iridessa was your ship."

"She is," Manny nodded, his hands lingering on her shoulders a beat longer than strictly necessary. "But she's in dry dock for routine maintenance. I'm temporarily commanding the Aurelia rather than taking shore leave."

His gaze shifted to include her companions. "Julia and Seren! Wonderful to see you both again."

"You as well." Julia offered sincerely.

"I apologize, I do not have much time now," He checked his watch: a vintage timepiece with a worn leather band. "We sail in forty minutes. But, please, join me for dinner tonight at the captain's table, I insist."

"We'd be delighted," Seren answered before Tessa could formulate a response.

Manny smiled broadly, his eyes crinkling at the corners. "Eight o'clock at Le Jardin d'Or, yes?"

With a last lingering look at Tessa, the captain strode away, crew members parting respectfully as he passed.

"Well, well, well," Seren linked her arm through Tessa's as they continued toward the elevators. "Captain Delicious was not on our itinerary."

"He's just an acquaintance from the last cruise," Tessa protested, though her cheeks burned tellingly.

"An acquaintance who kisses you hello and makes you blush like a schoolgirl?"

Julia pressed the elevator button. "That's quite the acquaintance. Besides, I recall the two of you spending quite a bit of time together on the Iridessa."

"Your face is positively glowing," Seren added. "Like you've been standing too close to a fire."

"It's warm in here," Tessa muttered as they stepped into the elevator.

The doors were about to close when a hand shot between them. They slid open again to reveal a striking young woman with dark hair twisted into a sleek knot, wearing crisp linen trousers and an elegant blouse.

"Mom!"

"Kelly?" Tessa's eyes widened in genuine shock. "What on earth?"

Kelly Monroe stepped into the elevator, her sharp eyes taking in the scene.

"Surprise! Did you really think I'd let you celebrate retirement without me?"

"But your work, I thought you couldn't get away." Tessa embraced her daughter, joy and confusion mingling on her face.

"I rearranged some meetings and handed off a project." Kelly returned the hug before nodding to Julia and Seren. "Hi, Aunt Julia, Aunt Seren."

As the elevator ascended, Kelly explained how she'd booked the cruise on impulse after Tessa mentioned it during their last call. "I really wanted to celebrate your retirement with you. Plus, I've been working too much. Eleven days unplugged sounds perfect."

* * *

Tessa's suite was bathed in the soft glow of early evening filtering through the balcony doors as she applied a final touch of mascara. The Mediterranean sunset painted the room in amber hues, catching the sequins on her navy cocktail dress and sending tiny prismatic reflections dancing across the walls.

"Are you almost ready? We'll be more than fashionably late at this rate," Seren called from the sitting area, where she lounged on a plush sofa beside Julia.

Kelly paced near the balcony doors, occasionally glancing at her mother's reflection in the vanity mirror. "I still don't understand why dinner with the captain is such a big deal. Don't they do that with all the passengers?"

"Not every passenger gets a personal invitation directly from the captain," Julia murmured, exchanging a knowing look with Seren.

Tessa stood, smoothing her dress over her hips. The fabric draped elegantly, neither too formal nor too casual, exactly the impression she'd spent forty minutes perfecting. "How do I look?"

"Stunning," Julia answered.

"Like a woman with plans," Seren added with a mischievous smile.

"I need to use the restroom before we go," Kelly announced, disappearing into the marble-tiled bathroom.

Tessa turned to her friends. "Do you think this is too much? The dress, I mean. I don't want to seem like I'm trying too…"

"It's perfect," Julia assured her. "Casually elegant."

"And Captain Delgado won't know what hit him," Seren added with a wink.

The bathroom door opened, and Kelly emerged with something in her hand. "Mom, what's this…?" She held up a white prescription tube, squinting at the label.

Tessa's face flushed instantly. "Kelly Monroe! Were you going through my things?"

"It was right there on the counter," Kelly defended, still examining the container.

"Estradiol vaginal cream?" Her eyes widened in realization. "Mom, isn't this…"

"You know perfectly well what it is," Tessa snapped, crossing the room and plucking the tube from her daughter's hand. "And you should also know better than to invade my privacy."

Kelly's analytical mind was already connecting dots. "But that's prescribed for…" she hesitated, seemingly uncomfortable with the direction of her thoughts. "That's usually for women who are… sexually active."

The room fell silent. Julia suddenly found her manicure fascinating, while Seren bit her lip to keep a smile from breaking out.

"Yes," Tessa replied simply, tucking the tube into a drawer. "It is."

Kelly's mouth opened, then closed, then opened again. "But you just got divorced."

"I got divorced almost three months ago," Tessa corrected.

"Are you seeing someone?" Kelly's protective instincts visibly flared.

Tessa sighed, meeting her daughter's gaze directly. "Not currently."

"But why would you need…" Kelly's face contorted as understanding dawned.

"Because it had been a while," Tessa said matter-of-factly. "Your father and I hadn't been intimate for nearly three years before I left. Dr. Patel suggested it might be helpful when I was ready to re-enter the dating world."

Julia and Seren exchanged glances, silent laughter dancing in their eyes.

"I just…" Kelly stammered, blushing. "I never thought…"

"That your mother might want a sex life post-divorce?" Tessa arched an eyebrow. "Darling, I'm sixty-two, not dead."

Seren finally lost her battle with composure, a snort of laughter escaping. "Sorry," she gasped. "But Kelly, you should see your face right now."

"It's just weird," Kelly muttered, visibly processing this new concept of her mother.

"No weirder than me finding your vibrator when you were in college," Tessa replied, applying a final touch of lipstick.

"Mom!" Kelly's horror was palpable.

Chapter 2

The maître d' led Tessa, Julia, Seren, and Kelly through Le Jardin d'Or's opulent entrance. Crystal chandeliers suspended from the high ceiling cast a golden glow over tables draped in cream-colored linens. Fresh arrangements of Mediterranean flowers—lavender, bougainvillea, and jasmine—adorned each table, their subtle fragrance mingling with the aromas of French cuisine. Floor-to-ceiling windows showcased the darkening Mediterranean waters, the last hints of sunset painting the horizon in fading oranges and purples.

Captain Delgado rose from his seat at the head of a large rectangular table as they approached. "Ah, the guests of honor have arrived," Captain Delgado announced, his smile warming as he made eye contact with Tessa.

She accepted the captain's gallant gesture as he pulled out the chair to his immediate right, positioning her as his special guest.

"Welcome, everyone," the captain said once they were settled. "I thought it would be lovely for some of our distinguished passengers to become acquainted early in our journey. Perhaps we could go around the table with brief introductions?"

When her turn came, Tessa spoke with practiced poise. "Tessa Monroe. Recently retired corporate attorney from Baltimore, Maryland, celebrating my new freedom with dear friends."

Julia followed with quiet confidence. "Julia Benton, retired accountant from Baltimore. I'm working on my first novel and hoping this voyage provides fresh inspiration."

"Seren Marwood," Seren announced with characteristic enthusiasm. "Owner of Marwood Travels and hostess of extraordinary retreats."

Kelly straightened almost imperceptibly when her turn came. "Kelly Monroe, Tessa's daughter. I'm a partner at Vertex Ventures in San Francisco, specializing in early-stage investments for tech startups focusing on sustainable energy and climate solutions." Her confidence seemed innate rather than practiced, the assurance of someone who knew her worth in any room.

Several more guests introduced themselves until the attention turned to a man seated directly across from Kelly. With an athletic build, dark hair touched with distinguished silver at the temples, and an easy smile, he commanded attention without seeming to try.

"Liam McDougal," he offered with a slight Scottish lilt. "Traveling solo on this voyage. I work in financial consulting." He paused, his gaze lingering on Kelly. "Actually, I've heard of Vertex. Impressive portfolio. You were involved in the Solar Stream funding round last year, weren't you?"

Kelly's eyebrow rose slightly. "We were. Though that wasn't widely publicized."

"I keep my ear to the ground," Liam replied with a casual shrug that somehow evaded further explanation.

As the first course arrived, a delicate scallop tartare with citrus and fennel—conversations bloomed around the table. The captain turned subtly toward Tessa, effectively creating a private space within the larger gathering.

"I am sorry I had to run off so quickly this afternoon." His apology extended to his eyes. "Embarkation day is always quite busy."

"I completely understand," Tessa demurred. "I am sure we will have time to catch up."

"The night is still young," Captain Delgado replied, his eyes conveying promises his position wouldn't allow him to voice openly.

Down the table, Kelly and Liam had fallen into an animated conversation about venture capital trends, their heads tilted toward each other with unmistakable interest.

"Solar Stream's approach to decentralized energy storage is genuinely revolutionary," Kelly was saying, her usual reserve giving way to passion. "But how exactly did you come to know about our involvement?"

Liam smiled enigmatically. "Let's just say I've developed good instincts for recognizing key players."

The meal progressed through expertly prepared courses: lobster bisque, herb-crusted lamb, and a chocolate soufflé that drew appreciative murmurs from around the table. Wine flowed freely, conversations deepened, and at every chance, Captain Delgado's hand brushed Tessa's.

Julia and Seren exchanged knowing glances but maintained their discretion. Kelly, absorbed in her discussion with Liam, missed the gestures entirely.

As coffee and digestifs were served, guests began making polite departures. The captain leaned close to Tessa's ear.

"I'm needed on the bridge for a while. Perhaps you'd care to join me? The night view of the Mediterranean is quite spectacular from there."

Tessa nodded, a small smile playing at her lips. "I'd like that."

Across the table, Kelly rose from her chair. "Liam suggested cocktails at the Luna di Mare Lounge. Anyone care to join us?"

Tessa noted the invitation was perfunctory at best; her daughter's attention was clearly fixed on her new acquaintance. "You two go ahead. I have other plans."

* * *

Julia and Seren found themselves alone as their party dispersed, Tessa with her captain and Kelly with her newfound companion. The two friends exchanged meaningful glances.

"Well," Seren said, her eyes twinkling with mischief, "it seems everyone's found evening entertainment but us."

Julia chuckled softly. "I can only imagine the kind of 'entertainment' Tessa might be enjoying right about now."

Seren winked. "I wouldn't mind a nightcap."

Julia shook her head. "How about the Aureate Lounge? I heard they have a wonderful pianist tonight."

The Aureate Lounge occupied a prime position on Deck 12, with floor-to-ceiling windows offering sweeping views of the darkened Mediterranean. Soft amber lighting cast a warm glow across the polished surfaces, creating an atmosphere of understated luxury. The space hummed with quiet conversation, punctuated by the delicate notes of a grand piano where a silver-haired woman played Debussy with remarkable sensitivity.

They selected a cozy seating area near the windows, where the vastness of the night sea stretched before them—an inky canvas scattered with distant lights from fishing boats and, far off, the glimmer of coastal towns.

"Pair of Spanish sherries: the Pedro Ximenez," Seren informed the server who appeared at their side.

As they settled into plush armchairs, Julia gazed out at the endless horizon. "Hard to believe Tessa and I are retired, and you are selling the business."

"We are entering the best season of our lives," Seren observed. "I, for one, am looking forward to it."

Before Julia could respond, a man approached their seating area. Tall with a trim physique, he carried himself with the easy confidence of someone accustomed to receiving positive attention. His tailored linen shirt and designer watch suggested comfortable wealth, while his smile, practiced yet effective, displayed perfect teeth.

"Ladies, forgive the intrusion. That view is spectacular, isn't it?" His voice carried a hint of what might have been a New England accent, smoothed by years of travel. "Would you mind if I joined you briefly? The lounge seems otherwise full."

It wasn't, but Seren gestured to an adjacent chair with characteristic generosity.

"Be our guest."

The man settled into the chair, placing his tumbler of amber liquid on the table. "Patrick Desmond."

"Seren Marwood. And this is Julia Benton."

"A pleasure." His eyes lingered just a fraction too long on each of them. "Are you traveling together?"

"With friends," Julia replied, taking a measured sip of her sherry.

"Ah, wonderful. Nothing like good company at sea." He leaned forward slightly. "And is this a special occasion? Anniversary perhaps?"

Seren laughed. "No husbands on this voyage."

Something flickered behind Patrick's eyes; interest suddenly sharpening. "I see. So, you ladies are traveling… independently?"

"With friends," Julia repeated more firmly.

"And do you cruise often? This is my third cruise this year." His smile widened. "I find it's the perfect way to meet interesting people."

Julia felt a familiar prickle of awareness. She'd spent decades reading people across negotiating tables, recognizing when questions weren't merely conversational but tactical.

"I'm afraid I'm not as interesting as you might hope," she said pleasantly but firmly. "I'm not single, just traveling without my partner."

Patrick pivoted smoothly toward Seren. "And you? Do you enjoy meeting new people on these voyages?"

Seren's smile remained fixed, but her eyes cooled. "I enjoy casual conversation, absolutely. But if you're fishing for something more, I should tell you I'm not in the market." She raised her glass in a small toast. "Though I appreciate good manners and directness."

Patrick's expression barely faltered, though something like irritation flashed briefly in his eyes. He drained his glass and stood. "Well, ladies, enjoy your evening. Perhaps we'll cross paths again."

They watched as he made his way across the lounge, settling into a chair near a woman sitting alone: silver-haired, elegant, wearing an expensive-looking sapphire pendant.

"Well," Seren murmured once he was out of earshot. "That didn't take long."

Julia nodded toward Patrick, now leaning attentively toward another woman.

"Think he's one of those cruise Casanovas, like we saw on the Iridessa?"

"Without question." Seren sipped her sherry. "Did you see that watch? Expensive but not quite right. And the way he was fishing for information…"

"Looking for lonely women with deep pockets," Julia agreed. "Poor thing he's talking to now has no idea what she's in for."

* * *

Up on the bridge, the soft glow of instrument panels cast a blue-green luminescence across the darkened command center. Officers moved with quiet efficiency, their voices low as they monitored systems and checked course headings. Captain Delgado stood at the center of this choreographed routine, radiating calm authority as he reviewed the night's navigation plan.

"Steady on course two-two-zero, Mr. Ramirez. Weather report?"

"Clear conditions expected through tomorrow evening, Captain. Light winds from the southeast, five to seven knots."

Manny nodded, initialing the log before turning his attention to the bridge wing where Tessa stood silhouetted against the night. Her elegant figure was perfectly still; face turned toward the distant shimmer of Valletta's lights, a constellation of human-made stars fading steadily as Aurelia pulled away from Malta's shores.

He watched her for several moments, noting something different about her posture, a certain tension gone from her shoulders, replaced by something lighter, more fluid. The Tessa Monroe he'd met a year ago had been striking, confident, and entirely self-contained. This woman seemed somehow more present, as though she'd shed a layer of armor.

"Everything secure, Mr. Ramirez. I'll be on the bridge wing if needed."

Manny crossed to where Tessa stood, the metal door sealing with a pneumatic hiss behind him. The night air carried hints of salt and distant land.

"Penny for your thoughts?" he asked, joining her at the railing.

Tessa drew in a deep breath and released it slowly, as though exhaling a year's worth of complications. "I was just thinking about how much has changed since I was last aboard one of your ships."

"Good changes, I hope?"

"Mostly." She turned toward him, her silver hair catching the moonlight. "I finalized my divorce. Sold the house, the one with the ridiculous fountain James insisted on installing. Retired from the firm after thirty years."

Manny leaned against the railing. "That's quite a year."

"Julia's been a godsend through it all. When she moved to the Eastern Shore to be with Reid, she let me lease her condo." Tessa's laugh was soft, almost private. "It's temporary, just until I figure out what comes next. But it's been a safe harbor."

"And have you? Figured out what comes next?"

She shook her head. "No. That's partly why I'm here."

Manny studied her profile, the elegant lines of her face illuminated by starlight.

She seemed both more vulnerable and more powerful than the woman he'd met before, a paradox that only enhanced her allure.

"Walk with me?" he offered, gesturing toward the officers' deck that curved around the ship's bow.

They strolled in comfortable silence, the gentle vibration of the engines beneath their feet, the vast Mediterranean stretching black and limitless before them. Crew members they passed nodded respectfully, then discreetly averted their eyes.

"There's a small lounge just ahead," Manny said eventually. "Private. Quiet."

The officers' lounge was deserted, its leather chairs arranged around low tables, a small bar stocked with premium spirits. Through panoramic windows, the sea and stars melded into a single canvas of darkness and light.

"Nightcap?" he asked, moving behind the bar.

"Bourbon, if you have it."

He poured two fingers of amber liquid into crystal tumblers. "Ice?"

"Neat."

They settled into adjacent chairs, angled toward the windows. The ship cut silently through darkness, the only evidence of movement the occasional swell of waves against the hull.

Tessa took a sip of bourbon. "How did you end up on the Aurelia? I thought you were captaining the Iridessa."

Manny's gaze turned thoughtful, his eyes drifting momentarily to the darkness beyond the windows before returning to her.

"Due to some unexpected circumstances, the other captain had to be replaced," he explained carefully. "The company needed someone who could take over quickly, and I happened to be on shore leave. Sometimes life has its own navigation charts."

"I'm glad it worked out this way," Tessa admitted, her voice warm with sincerity.

They traded stories as their glasses emptied, the conversation flowing without effort, punctuated by laughter and moments of comfortable silence.

"I've missed this," Manny said quietly.

"Bourbon?"

"Conversation that doesn't involve navigational charts or fuel efficiency." His eyes held hers. "With you, specifically."

The air between them shifted, charged with possibility.

"I get a full day off when we dock in Porto Cervo," he said, leaning forward slightly.

"You do?"

"I'd like to show you Porto Cervo, not the tourist version, but my own. The hidden coves, the family restaurants where no one speaks

English, the views that don't make it onto postcards." His voice dropped lower. "Would you join me?"

Tessa considered him for a long moment. The bourbon had left a pleasant warmth in her chest, but her thoughts remained clear. This man, perceptive, patient, with eyes that saw her completely, represented a path she hadn't planned on.

"I'd like that," she said finally. "Very much."

Something like relief crossed Manny's face. "Good. Excellent."

"Now." She set down her empty glass and stood. "I should get back. Kelly will be wondering where I've disappeared to."

Manny walked her to the elevator that would return her to the passenger decks. As the doors opened, he took her hand, his thumb brushing across her knuckles.

Chapter 3

Seren led Julia, Tessa, and Kelly down the gangway and off the Aurelia onto Sicilian soil under a brilliant azure sky promising a perfect day in Catania.

"Private car should be right over there," Seren said, scanning the row of vehicles waiting beyond the terminal. She waved when she spotted a sleek black Mercedes with a distinguished-looking driver holding a sign that read "Marwood."

The driver, a Sicilian with salt-and-pepper hair and an elegant manner, greeted them with practiced formality. "Signore, welcome to Catania. I am Antonio, your guide for today."

Julia settled into the plush leather seat with a contented sigh. "Seren, you've outdone yourself with this excursion."

"Wait until you see what I've arranged," Seren beamed, her eyes glinting with mischief. "The Bronte pistachio groves are absolutely divine. They're grown on volcanic soil from Mount Etna that gives them a flavor you can't find anywhere else."

Kelly's head snapped up. "Pistachios? As in nuts?"

"Yes, darling. The finest in the world." Seren paused, registering Kelly's expression. "Oh! Your nut allergy. I completely forgot."

"The tour centers around pistachio tasting," Kelly said, her voice rising slightly. "I'll just stand around watching everyone else eat?"

Tessa touched her daughter's arm. "I'm sure we can…"

"Kelly, darling," Seren cut in with a theatrical wave of her bejeweled hand, "you were a surprise addition to our little group. The itinerary was set months ago. You'll just have to abstain and enjoy the scenery."

A beat of silence hung in the car before Kelly's lips twitched. "So, I'm just supposed to breathe in all those nutty fumes and hope I don't swell up like a pufferfish?"

"Think of it as character building," Seren replied, reaching across to pat Kelly's knee.

The tension broke as Kelly burst into laughter. "Only you could get away with almost killing me and making it sound like my fault."

"I specialize in audacity, darling. It's kept me alive through three husbands."

The car wound its way through Catania's streets, passing ornate Baroque buildings before climbing the slopes of Mount Etna. Antonio pointed out landmarks, his accent thick but his English impeccable.

"Speaking of specialties," Julia said, turning to Tessa with a knowing smile. "You never told us how your evening with the handsome captain concluded."

Tessa kept her eyes fixed on the passing landscape. "We had a nightcap and talked."

"That's it? 'Talked'?" Seren pressed, her voice laced with friendly skepticism. "You disappeared for hours to 'talk'?"

"Yes, we talked," Tessa insisted, though a small smile played at the corners of her mouth. "About the cruise, about life, about his adventures at sea."

"Your face says there was more than talking," Kelly observed, studying her mother with keen interest.

"Since when are you the relationship expert?" Tessa countered lightly.

"Since I watched you float back to the cabin around midnight looking like you'd drunk too much Red Bull, and you had wings."

The car rounded a bend, revealing terraced hillsides covered in short, bushy trees laden with clusters of red-hulled pistachios. Antonio slowed the vehicle as they approached an elegant stone farmhouse.

"We're here, Signore. Azienda Agricola Gabriele, home of the finest pistachios in Sicily."

As they exited the car, Seren linked her arm through Tessa's. "Don't think we're letting you off the hook that easily."

Julia joined them on Tessa's other side. "What else happened with Manny?"

Tessa sighed, knowing resistance was futile with these three. "If you must know, he asked me to join him in Porto Cervo. It's his day off."

"A date?" Kelly asked, suddenly paying full attention.

Tessa thought for a moment. "Yes, I guess it is. He wants to show me the local side of the island, away from tourists."

"The local side of the island," Seren repeated with exaggerated significance. "Is that what they're calling it these days?"

"Mom has a date," Kelly said, her voice a mixture of surprise and something harder to identify.

"Is it so hard to believe a man actually wants to spend time with me?" Tessa asked.

"A man," Julia echoed, "who has been carrying a torch for you since last year."

"And who looks at you like you're the only star in his sky," Seren added.

Before Tessa could respond, they were greeted by a smiling Italian woman who ushered them toward the pistachio groves. Kelly hung back slightly, watching her mother laugh at something Julia whispered.

"Don't worry," Seren said, noticing Kelly's expression. "We had them prepare special non-pistachio treats just for you. I wasn't really going to let you starve while we indulged."

"I'm not worried about the nuts," Kelly said quietly.

"Ah." Seren nodded, understanding immediately. "You're worried about your mother's heart. Trust me, darling, sometimes the things we don't plan for turn out to be exactly what we need."

* * *

The morning sun climbed higher as they wandered through the terraced groves. Julia lagged behind the group, incessantly snapping photos with her phone. She captured the gnarled pistachio trees against the volcanic landscape, close-ups of the reddish husks, and candid shots of her friends sampling pistachio-infused delicacies. Every few minutes, she'd pause to jot notes in a small leather-bound notebook she kept tucked in her purse.

"More writing inspiration?" Tessa asked, doubling back to join her.

Julia nodded, her eyes bright with enthusiasm. "The way the light filters through these trees against Etna's silhouette? Pure magic. I'm thinking of setting a scene here for my new protagonist."

"Should I be worried I'll end up as a character in your next novel?" Tessa laughed.

"Only the best parts," Julia winked, scribbling another note before tucking the notebook away.

Ahead of them, Seren walked with their guide, peppering him with questions about the property's accommodation potential and nearby attractions. Her animated gestures and intense focus revealed her mind was already calculating possibilities.

"She's scouting again," Tessa observed.

"Perpetually," Julia agreed. "She mentioned wanting to expand her retreat offerings into Sicily. Something about 'volcanic energy and ancient wisdom.'"

When they rejoined the others near a stone wall overlooking the countryside, Kelly was engrossed in her device, thumbs flying across the screen, her brow furrowed in concentration.

"No, absolutely not," Kelly said into her phone a few moments later, voice clipped and professional. "The valuation doesn't support those terms. They need to come down at least fifteen percent, or we walk."

Tessa exchanged a knowing glance with Julia as their guide discreetly stepped away to give Kelly privacy.

"Tell Wu I'll call him back after I review the latest projections," Kelly finished, ending the call with a sigh. "Sorry. Crisis averted. For now."

"Darling, we're standing in paradise, and you're haggling over percentages," Tessa said, gesturing to the breathtaking panorama of countryside and distant sea.

"That 'haggling' just saved my fund about four million dollars," Kelly replied, though she did pocket her phone. "Some of us aren't retired yet."

"Some of us worked ourselves into bad marriages and missed watching our children grow up," Tessa countered gently. "Work will still be there tomorrow."

Kelly's expression softened. "I know, Mom. It's just…"

"A tough habit to break," Tessa finished for her. "I remember."

Their chauffeur appeared at the edge of the grove, signaling it was time to continue their journey. As they piled back into the car, Seren was practically vibrating with excitement.

"The owner is willing to discuss exclusive booking rights for two weeks next spring," she announced. "Perfect timing for my 'Awaken Your Inner Goddess' retreat series."

"Is that the one where middle-aged women dance naked under the full moon?" Kelly asked dryly.

"Only if they want to, darling. It's entirely optional."

"With Seren, nakedness is always optional," Julia murmured, earning a playful swat from her friend.

At lunchtime, they were seated at a pristine, white-clothed table on the terrace of Ristorante Sapio, the Michelin-starred jewel of Catania. Mount Etna loomed in the background, a silent guardian over their feast of seafood crudo, handmade pasta with sardines and wild fennel, and local wines that tasted of sunshine and salt air.

Kelly's phone buzzed again. She glanced at it, then reluctantly turned it face down.

"Progress," Tessa approved, raising her wine glass in salute.

"Speaking of progress," Seren said, leaning toward Kelly with mischievous intent, "how's your love life, darling? Anyone special warming your bed in San Francisco?"

Kelly nearly choked on her wine. "Subtle as ever, Aunt Seren."

"Life's too short for subtlety. You're thirty-seven, gorgeous, and successful. Please tell me you're not wasting that glorious body on spreadsheets alone."

"My love life is fine," Kelly said defensively.

"Really?" Tessa challenged. "All you ever talk to me about is work."

Kelly's silence was answer enough.

"Work isn't everything," Tessa said softly. "I learned that too late."

"I'm not you, Mom." Kelly's voice held an edge. "My career makes me happy."

"So did mine, until one day it didn't. Until I realized I'd built an empire and had no one to share it with."

The waiter arrived with the next course, momentarily diffusing the tension.

"All I'm saying," Seren continued after he'd departed, "is that life needs balance. Work, play, and a good tumble between the sheets occasionally."

Julia raised an eyebrow. "If Kelly's not careful, she'll end up needing her own prescription for Estradiol."

"Aunt Julia!" Kelly exclaimed, mortified.

"What? It's a perfectly normal medication for women who aren't regularly…"

"Can we please not discuss my hypothetical vaginal atrophy over lunch?" Kelly interrupted, though a reluctant smile tugged at her lips.

"Cheers to that," Tessa laughed, raising her glass again. "To less work, more play, and keeping our vaginas happy, by whatever means necessary."

Their glasses clinked in agreement as laughter rippled across the table, sweeter than any dessert the chef could prepare.

* * *

The afternoon passed in a pleasant haze as their private excursion continued through Taormina's winding streets and ancient ruins. The Greco-Roman amphitheater left them breathless, not just from the climb, but from the sweeping vistas of coastline and the imposing silhouette of Mount Etna against the sky.

As the day's warmth began to soften into evening, they found themselves in the charming hilltop village of Castelmola at the infamous Bar Turrisi. The establishment's unique décor revealed itself immediately, phalluses of every size, material, and configuration adorned the walls, tables, and even the door handles.

"Well," Julia said, settling into her chair, "I think we've found Seren's spiritual home."

Seren grinned, lifting her glass of almond wine. "I've always appreciated directness in interior design."

Kelly, for the first time all day, seemed genuinely present. She'd only reached for her phone a handful of times since lunch, a minor miracle by anyone's count. Even now, as she took a selfie with the bar's most prominent decorative element looming behind her, she seemed relaxed.

"Who's the lucky recipient of that particularly classy shot?" Tessa asked, eyebrows raised.

Kelly's fingers paused over the screen. "Just a friend back home. They'll appreciate the… artistic merit."

"I'm sure they will," Tessa said, not entirely convinced but pleased to see her daughter smiling genuinely.

The sweet almond wine flowed freely as they watched the sun begin its descent, casting golden light across ancient stones. Their conversation drifted from memories of past trips to dreams of future adventures. For a perfect moment, all four women existed in complete harmony, generations bridged by laughter and friendship.

Tessa's attention drifted to a couple seated near the terrace edge. She recognized the man immediately, one of the suspected lotharios from the ship, his salt-and-pepper hair artfully tousled, his attentions lavished on a woman Tessa had seen dining alone the previous evening.

"Don't look now," Tessa murmured, "but isn't that one of the lounge lizards we saw on the ship?"

Julia and Seren turned with all the subtlety of weather vanes in a hurricane.

"Oh, that's the one we saw chatting up a different woman last night," Seren confirmed. "Looks like he's found more prey."

They watched as the waiter delivered the check. The lothario made a show of reaching for his wallet, but his movements were deliberately slow, his expression expectant. Sure enough, the woman quickly produced her credit card with a dismissive wave of her hand.

"Did you see that?" Tessa whispered indignantly. "He didn't even pretend to argue."

"Professional gigolo," Julia assessed. "Classic technique."

Kelly snorted. "That explains why I saw him picking up a Viagra prescription at the pharmacy earlier. I had to go in for some ointment after that pistachio rash."

She gestured to a faint red patch on her wrist.

"Wait… he was getting Viagra?" Seren asked with a chuckle, suddenly interested.

"Well, at least he's committed to providing full service."

The women erupted in laughter, drawing curious glances from nearby tables.

"I don't see what's so funny," Tessa said, her brow furrowed. "These men prey on vulnerable women; they're con artists."

"Oh, Mom," Kelly sighed. "Those 'vulnerable women' are grown adults making their own choices. If Grandma Jenkins wants to bankroll some Mediterranean action during her golden years, who are we to judge?"

"It's predatory," Tessa insisted. "I should talk to Manny about it. The cruise line should warn people."

"Warn them about what?" Seren asked. "Attractive men seeking mutually beneficial arrangements? That's half the allure of cruising for some women."

Tessa shook her head, unconvinced. "There's something not right about it. And speaking of Manny…" She glanced at her watch. "I should head back. We are having cocktails tonight."

"Another date?" Julia teased.

"It's not a date," Tessa protested, though the blush creeping across her cheeks suggested otherwise. "It's just drinks."

"Just drinks," Seren repeated with a wink. "Well, he is a tall glass of something smooth and potent."

Chapter 4

The ship's towering hull gleamed against the late afternoon sun as Tessa and her companions approached the gangway. The four women were still chatting animatedly about their day in Catania, Kelly now walking beside her mother rather than trailing behind with her face buried in her phone.

As Tessa swiped her key card at security, a uniformed crew member stepped forward. His expression was professionally neutral, but there was an urgency in his stance.

"Mrs. Monroe? I apologize for the interruption. Captain Delgado requested for you to see him immediately. He says it's urgent."

Julia, Seren, and Kelly exchanged significant glances.

"So much for 'just drinks,'" Seren whispered to Julia.

"Is everything alright?" Tessa asked, a flutter of concern rising in her chest.

"The captain didn't specify, ma'am. If you'll follow me, please."

Tessa turned to her companions. "I'll catch up with you all later."

"Don't worry about us," Julia said with a knowing smile. "Take your time."

The crewman led Tessa through a series of corridors and up a private elevator that required his keycard. Minutes later, she found herself outside the captain's office, her mind racing with possibilities.

When the door opened, Manny's broad shoulders and silver hair came into view. He was pacing but stopped immediately when he saw her.

"Tessa! Thank you for coming so quickly." His accent thickened with what seemed like relief. "I apologize for the urgency and for interrupting your return."

"What's happened?" Tessa asked, stepping into the wood-paneled office.

"I have a… how do you say… a situation." He ran a hand through his hair. "Tonight, I am hosting a private dinner for diamond-level guests. Usually, my cruise director, she co-hosts with me, and she is much better at these things, but she is ill with a terrible stomach virus."

Understanding dawned on Tessa's face. "And you need a replacement."

"Yes!" Manny's eyes lit up. "I thought immediately of you. Your charm, your grace, your ability with people… would you consider helping me tonight? Make the small talk, charm them a little? I would be eternally grateful."

Tessa felt a mixture of flattery and trepidation. "When is this dinner?"

Manny glanced at his watch and winced. "Two hours from now?"

"Two hours!" Tessa's eyebrows shot up. "That doesn't give me much time to prepare."

"I know, I know." His hands gestured apologetically. "I waited too long, hoping Sophia would recover. You would be saving me, Tessa."

Something in his expression, a blend of hope and vulnerability beneath all that authority, made it impossible to refuse.

"Alright," she said, a small smile playing on her lips. "I'll do it."

The relief that washed over his face was immediate and genuine. "Grazie, bella. You are an angel."

* * *

Tessa's fingers flew across her phone screen as she made her way back to her suite, thumbs tapping out a hasty message to the group. She needed reinforcements. By the time she swiped her key card, her heart was hammering with equal parts excitement and panic.

She pushed open the door to find Julia sitting on the small sofa in a bathrobe, hair wrapped in a towel, while Seren was barefoot in yoga pants and a flowing tunic, mid-stretch. Kelly appeared from the bathroom in a bathrobe, her face slathered with cream.

"What's the emergency?" Seren's arms dropped to her sides. "You look like you've either seen a ghost or been propositioned."

Tessa dropped her handbag on the bed and paced the cabin. "Manny needs me to co-host a formal dinner with him tonight. The cruise director has a stomach virus, and he needs someone to help entertain the diamond-level guests."

"That's the emergency?" Julia unwrapped her towel, revealing damp hair. "I thought someone had fallen overboard."

"You don't understand." Tessa collapsed onto the edge of the bed. "It's in two hours. Two hours! After a day of wine tasting and traipsing around Catania in the heat, I look like something the cat dragged in. My head's fuzzy, my feet ache, and I haven't prepared a single thing to say to these people."

Kelly disappeared into the bathroom, returning seconds later without the cream.

"Mom, this is literally what you did for years… schmoozed with clients and made them feel important while negotiating deals."

"That was different. That was business." Tessa pressed her palms against her temples. "This is… I don't know what this is."

"This is Manny showing everyone the woman he's interested in," Seren said with a wicked grin. She rummaged through her handbag and produced a small tin. "Here—two aspirins and then straight into a cool bath. Not cold… cool. And drink this entire bottle of water before you start getting ready."

Julia was already heading to the bathroom. "I'll run the bath. Kelly, start looking through your mother's closet for something appropriate."

Twenty minutes later, Tessa lay in the tub, a cold compress on her forehead and cucumber-infused eye patches that Seren swore would "de-puff even the most exhausted eyes."

"These are organic," Seren called through the partially open bathroom door. "Made by some Zen master herbalist in a mountain village in Japan. They're miracles."

"They smell like a salad," Tessa murmured, but kept them in place.

In the main cabin, Kelly was creating a war zone of rejected outfits on the bed. "Too casual… too somber… too holiday… too trying-too-hard…" She muttered assessments as she slid hangers across the closet rod. "Ah! Perfect."

She pulled out a midnight blue cocktail dress with a subtle shimmer that caught the light as it moved. The neckline was elegant without being revealing, the length appropriate but still showing off Tessa's legs.

"Who would have thought I'd be helping my mother dress for a date?" Kelly mused, laying out the dress.

"It's not a date," Tessa called from the bathroom. "It's a professional favor."

"Keep telling yourself that," three voices chorused back.

By the time Tessa stood before the full-length mirror, the transformation was complete. The dress hugged her figure perfectly, her silver-gray bob gleamed under the cabin lights, and her skin had a healthy glow that belied her earlier exhaustion. Julia found a delicate silver necklace that drew attention to Tessa's collarbones, while Seren's miracle eye patches had indeed worked their magic.

"I don't know if I can do this," Tessa said, smoothing the dress nervously. "These diamond-level guests, they're probably all sophisticated world travelers who'll see right through me."

Kelly stood behind her mother, hands on Tessa's shoulders as they both looked in the mirror. "Mom, these are the exact same people you've been impressing your entire career. Wealthy, entitled, and desperately in need of someone to make them feel special for an evening. You've got this."

"She's right," Julia added. "And unlike those corporate dinners where you were working, tonight you get to enjoy yourself. With a very handsome captain, I might add."

Tessa's eyes met her own reflection, confident, elegant, ready. For the first time in years, perhaps decades, she was stepping into an evening purely for herself, not for a client or her now ex-husband or anyone else.

"Well," she said with a slow smile spreading across her face, "I suppose there are worse ways to spend an evening at sea."

* * *

Tessa arrived at Le Jardin d'Or exactly seven minutes early. She paused at the entrance, taking a steadying breath that did little to calm the flutter in her stomach. From behind the maître d's podium, Manny spotted her, and his face transformed. The professional captain's demeanor melted into something warmer, more personal.

"Tessa," he called, crossing the restaurant in long strides. He took both her hands in his, squeezing gently. "You look magnificent. And thank you again for this enormous favor."

"Happy to help," she replied, surprised at how steady her voice sounded when her legs felt like they might give way beneath her. The midnight blue dress caught the light as she moved, creating the illusion of stars against a dark sky.

Manny leaned closer, his voice dropping to a conspiratorial whisper. "These diamond-level guests, they can be… demanding. But with you here, they will be too charmed to complain about anything."

"Flattery will get you everywhere, Captain." She smiled, easing naturally into the role she'd played countless times during her career: confident, capable, the perfect hostess.

"The first guests should arrive at any moment," Manny said, glancing at his watch. "Shall we have a quick toast before they do?" He signaled to a passing server, who promptly delivered two flutes of champagne.

"To unexpected partnerships," Manny said, his eyes never leaving hers as they clinked glasses.

The first couple arrived moments later—elderly German aristocrats who immediately warmed to Tessa's genuine interest in their extensive travels. Within twenty minutes, the private section of the restaurant filled with diamond-level guests, a collection of wealth and privilege from around the world.

Tessa moved among them with practiced ease, making introductions, directing them toward the private dining area with its panoramic ocean views, ensuring everyone had their preferred drink. She remembered names effortlessly, noted personal details for future conversation, and subtly guided the social dynamics of the room, placing the talkative Swiss banker near the reserved Japanese CEO, steering the boisterous American tech mogul toward the equally energetic Brazilian heiress.

From across the room, Manny caught her eye and raised an eyebrow in appreciation. She responded with a small, private smile. Later, as she guided an elderly couple to their seats, he winked at her over their heads and heat bloomed across her chest that had nothing to do with the room's temperature.

Just as everyone was about to be seated, another couple arrived. Manny introduced the couple as Richard and Gloria.

"Captain Delgado," the man extended his hand with practiced charm. "Thank you for accommodating our last-minute change of plans."

"Of course, Mr. Collier. May I introduce Tessa Monroe, my co-host this evening."

Richard Collier's eyes flickered with recognition as he took Tessa's hand. "Pleasure to meet you, Mrs. Monroe." He greeted her with a heavy New York accent.

"Ms. Monroe," Tessa corrected, maintaining her professional smile. "I believe I saw you this morning."

A flash of discomfort crossed Richard's face before his smile reasserted itself. "Indeed. Gloria and I were exploring the local culture."

Gloria, a well-preserved woman in her seventies with expertly colored blonde hair and an expensive emerald pendant, beamed at Richard. "He's been the most wonderful tour guide. He knows all the hidden gems."

Manny directed them to the two empty seats at the large round table, and the dinner service began. Wine flowed freely as the first course arrived, a delicate seafood terrine that sparked appreciative murmurs around the table.

During a lull in conversation, Tessa turned to Richard and Gloria. "How long have you been married?"

Gloria placed her hand over Richard's. "We met just last night. There was an immediate connection, wasn't there, Richard?"

"Absolutely," Richard agreed, though Tessa noted his smile didn't quite reach his eyes. "Gloria and I have become fast friends."

"And what do you do, Richard?" Tessa pressed, cutting into her terrine. "For work, I mean."

"I'm a lifestyle consultant," he replied smoothly. "Mainly in Europe and the U.S. My work allows me to travel extensively."

"How convenient," Tessa remarked. "And how did you two meet exactly?"

Gloria enthusiastically took over. "I was having trouble with the app for shore excursions, and Richard offered to help. We got to talking, and, well, he's such wonderful company. So knowledgeable about everything—art, wine, history."

Across the table, Manny caught Tessa's eye and gave her a subtle look, half warning, half question. He smoothly interjected, "Speaking of wine, our sommelier has selected a special vintage to complement the next course. It comes from a small vineyard near my hometown in Italy."

The conversation pivoted as Manny shared stories of his childhood in coastal Italy, expertly drawing attention away from Richard and Gloria. As glasses were refilled and the main course arrived, Tessa caught the grateful glance Richard shot toward the captain.

Tessa didn't miss the subtle exchange between Manny and Richard—that look of understanding that passed between them, the slight nod Richard gave in return. A cold uneasiness settled in her stomach as she sipped her wine, maintaining her pleasant hostess smile while her mind raced.

How well did Manny know Richard? Was that intervention to redirect the conversation merely social grace, or something more calculated? The thought that Manny might be aware of, perhaps even facilitating, these lotharios' activities aboard his ship disturbed her deeply.

She recalled the man Julia and Seren had encountered in the lounge, working his way through single women. Was this some sort of unofficial cruise service? Wealthy women paired with charming men who knew exactly what to say and how to say it?

As Manny regaled the table with another charming anecdote about Italian coastal life, Tessa studied his face. Those kind eyes, the genuine warmth she'd felt from him… had she misread everything? Was this man she found herself increasingly drawn to orchestrating romantic predators across his fleet?

When Manny caught her watching him, his smile faltered slightly at her cool assessment. He raised a questioning eyebrow, but Tessa merely turned to engage the couple beside her, her heart heavy with suspicion.

Chapter 5

Tessa, Seren, and Julia set off early from the ship, the sky still holding the golden hues of morning. The sea air tasted different here, sweeter somehow, infused with the essence of Capri's wild herbs and flowers. Their private driver navigated the winding roads with practiced ease, pointing out landmarks as they climbed higher into the hills of Anacapri.

"Kelly texted," Tessa said, glancing at her phone. "She and Liam are heading to the Blue Grotto. Apparently, he knows someone who can get them in before the crowds."

"Of course he does," Julia replied with a knowing smile. "That man seems to 'know someone' everywhere."

Seren leaned forward, her collection of silver bracelets jingling. "I'd rather see this olive grove than another tourist trap anyway. Real places, real people, that's where the magic happens."

The car rounded a final curve, revealing an iron gate flanked by ancient stone pillars. Beyond stretched a sea of silver-green, olive trees standing in orderly rows across the terraced hillside. The driver pulled to a stop in a small gravel clearing where a man waited, his weathered face breaking into a welcoming smile.

"Benvenuti a Tenuta delle Ombre d'Argento," he said, his English carrying a melodic Italian lilt. "I am Matteo Rossi. Welcome to my family's home."

Matteo led them through the grove, explaining the cultivation methods that had remained largely unchanged for generations. His hands moved expressively as he spoke, occasionally brushing a trunk or leaf with familiar affection.

"Some of these trees are over two hundred years old," he explained. "My great-grandfather's great-grandfather tended them. We still press the olives using traditional methods, though we have made a few concessions to modern times," he added with a wink.

While Tessa and Julia listened attentively, Seren's attention was captured by the villa that rose above the trees at the heart of the property. Its faded grandeur called to her, and as soon as there was a pause in Matteo's narrative, she pointed toward it.

"That building, it's extraordinary. Is it part of your estate?"

Matteo's expression softened with something like regret. "Sì, the Villa delle Ombre. Once the pride of the estate, now…" He gestured vaguely. "Time and economics are not always kind to old beauties."

"May we see it?" Seren asked, already moving in that direction.

As they approached, the villa's true condition became apparent. Shutters hung askew, plaster crumbled from walls, and ivy claimed entire sections of the façade. Yet its bones remained magnificent, soaring ceilings, graceful arches, and expansive terraces offering breathtaking views of the sea and mountains.

"This could be incredible," Seren breathed, spinning in what must have once been a grand salon. Her mind raced with possibilities. "Imagine yoga retreats here on this terrace at sunrise, art classes capturing that view. Cooking workshops using olive oil pressed right here on the property."

She moved from room to room, her enthusiasm growing. "This space could host meditation sessions. And this would make a perfect dining hall for communal meals."

Matteo followed, watching her with growing fascination. This vibrant woman with her flowing clothes and uninhibited energy saw what he had always seen—the villa's potential, not its decay.

"You have a beautiful vision, Signora Seren," he said. "But the cost to restore… it is prohibitive. The foundation needs reinforcement, the roof replacement, new plumbing, electricity…" His hands spread in a gesture of futility. "For a retreat center, the investment would be enormous, with uncertain return."

Seren paused at a window, framing a perfect view of the olive grove below. "But what a shame to let it waste away. Places like this have souls, Matteo. They're meant to be lived in, to witness human joy and connection."

While they talked, Julia wandered the grounds, notebook in hand, occasionally stopping to take photographs or jot down impressions. Every corner seemed to whisper stories… of harvest celebrations, of secret lovers meeting on moonlit terraces, of families gathering through generations of summers.

"I can see why you're drawn to it," Matteo said to Seren, their shoulders nearly touching as they looked out over his land. "You have the same spirit as the villa: bold, unapologetic." His eyes, warm and appreciative, met hers. "It is refreshing to meet someone who sees possibilities where others see only problems."

The morning concluded with a tasting at Matteo's cottage; fresh bread dipped in olive oils of varying intensities, accompanied by his family's wine and plates of local cheese.

"To new friends," Matteo proposed, raising his glass.

As they reluctantly prepared to leave, Seren took one last look at the villa, silhouetted against the brilliant blue sky. Something about it refused to let go of her imagination. Behind its crumbling walls, she sensed not just history, but potential, waiting, like a story not yet finished.

* * *

Their next stop, the Ristorante Pizzeria Aurora, buzzed with lunchtime energy, tourists and locals alike savoring wood-fired pizzas and panoramic views of Capri Town's meandering streets. Tessa, Julia, and Seren secured a prime table near the edge, where a gentle breeze carried the scent of basil and melted mozzarella.

"I could get used to this," Julia murmured, lifting her wineglass to capture the midday sunlight. She took a delicate sip of the local white, savoring its crisp minerality.

Tessa was about to reply when her attention snagged on a familiar profile across the piazza. "Don't be obvious, but look over my right shoulder. Isn't that another one from the ship?"

Seren tilted her sunglasses downward, peering over the rims with practiced subtlety. "The one in the navy linen shirt? Helping that woman with the enormous sunhat into the Mercedes?"

Julia twisted a strand of her silver-streaked hair, using the motion to mask her interest. "That's Eloise Whitman. Diamond-tier cruiser. I met her at the wine tasting yesterday. She mentioned something about a private tour with her new friend."

They watched as the man, tanned, fit, somewhere in his late fifties, placed a possessive hand at the small of Eloise's back, then leaned in to say something that made her laugh before helping her into the luxury sedan.

"That makes three we've spotted," Tessa said, her voice dropping. "Patrick Desmond, Richard Collier, and now him."

"Professional companions," Seren pronounced with authority, tearing a piece of pizza crust and dragging it through olive oil. "Gigolos, if you prefer the old-fashioned term."

"It must be quite profitable," Julia mused. "These Mediterranean cruises aren't cheap, and neither are private tours in every port."

Their waiter arrived with steaming plates of pasta, momentarily distracting them. When he departed, Tessa leaned forward conspiratorially.

"I wonder how it works. Do they book the cruise knowing wealthy single women will be aboard, or are they hired specifically by someone?"

"Both, probably," Seren said, twirling perfect spirals of spaghetti around her fork. "Some are freelancers hunting opportunities, others have arrangements through agencies."

"You sound suspiciously knowledgeable," Julia remarked with raised eyebrows.

Seren's laugh carried across the terrace, drawing admiring glances from nearby tables. "My third husband had a friend who did it part-time after his divorce. Called himself a 'travel companion for discerning ladies.' He made enough in tips and gifts to spend half the year in the Mediterranean and half in the Caribbean."

"And the women know what they're getting into?" Tessa asked. "These men seem pretty predatory to me."

"Usually. It's an unspoken arrangement. Companionship, security, someone photogenic for dinner and excursions." Seren paused, considering. "I'll admit, when I'm eighty and my knees can't handle cobblestones alone anymore, I might hire one myself."

Julia nearly choked on her wine. "You would not."

"I absolutely would," Seren insisted, utterly unapologetic. "Not for sex, though I'm not ruling anything out, but for convenience. Someone to handle luggage, to navigate unfamiliar places, and make me laugh. Seems like a perfectly reasonable expense."

"Like hiring a private tour guide who also offers arm-holding services?" Tessa suggested, amused.

"Exactly," Seren nodded. "Plus, having a handsome man gazing adoringly at you is good for the circulation."

They dissolved into laughter, drawing curious glances from nearby tables. When they recovered, Tessa's expression turned contemplative.

"You don't think Liam could be one of them, do you? He's been rather attentive to Kelly."

Julia carefully considered before answering. "I don't get that impression. There's something genuine about him."

"And he's hardly targeting the elderly widow demographic," Seren pointed out. "Kelly's successful but hardly the usual mark."

"You're right," Tessa conceded, though uncertainty lingered in her voice. "I just worry. Kelly works so hard, and I don't know when she was last in a relationship."

"Like mother, like daughter," Julia said gently.

Their conversation drifted to other topics as they finished their meal—the vibrant colors of the island, a particular ceramic shop Seren insisted they visit, Julia's growing collection of photographs that might inspire her writing.

As they wandered through Capri Town's narrow lanes afterward, sampling gelato and admiring the bougainvillea cascading over whitewashed walls, the earlier discussion faded beneath the island's spell. The Augustus Gardens offered breathtaking vistas of the Faraglioni rock formations jutting from the azure sea, and for a moment, all three women stood in appreciative silence.

Their tour concluded with a descent back to Marina Grande, where their tender waited to return them to the Aurelia. As they settled into seats on the open deck, Seren raised her face to the sun.

"I wonder what Captain Delgado has planned for your tour tomorrow," she teased, bumping Tessa's shoulder playfully.

"Let's hope it doesn't involve any gigolos," Tessa replied, but her smile betrayed her anticipation for whatever the day might bring.

* * *

Sunset painted the Aurelia's white hull in brilliant amber as Tessa, Seren, and Julia made their way back to the ship after their day in Capri. The trio walked up the gangway, pleasantly tired from exploring the island's winding paths and breathtaking vistas.

"I need a shower and about twelve hours of sleep," Julia announced, fanning herself with her sunhat.

"I need a martini," Seren countered. "The dirtier the better."

Tessa laughed, but a familiar figure suddenly caught her attention on the pool deck above. Captain Delgado stood near the railing in conversation with an elderly woman. The woman's tasteful jewelry and casual elegance spoke of old money and quiet refinement.

"You two go ahead," Tessa said. "I'll catch up with you at dinner."

Julia followed Tessa's gaze and raised an eyebrow. "Give the captain our regards."

As her friends continued toward the elevators, Tessa climbed the stairs to the pool deck. The setting sun cast long shadows across the polished teak as she approached, not wanting to interrupt but eager to say hello. She slowed as she drew near enough to hear their conversation.

"Are there others onboard?" Tessa heard the woman ask.

"There are two others," Manny replied.

"Interesting," was the only reply from the woman.

"I will make a personal introduction to Patrick Desmond," the captain continued, his voice carrying in the evening air. "I can arrange for you to have dinner together this evening, if you'd like."

"That's perfect," Vivian replied, her aristocratic British accent distinct. "I will look forward to it."

Tessa froze, her smile fading—Patrick Desmond, one of the Casanovas working the ship.

"I'll have my staff make the arrangements," Manny continued, unaware of her presence. "The Maraviglia restaurant at eight?"

"Perfect. Thank you for being so helpful, Captain." Vivian turned slightly and noticed Tessa standing there. "Oh! Hello there."

Manny spun around, surprise flashing across his face. "Tessa! I didn't see you."

"Clearly," she replied, her voice cooler than the Mediterranean breeze. She nodded politely to the woman.

"The captain was just helping me with my dining arrangements." The woman glanced at her diamond-encrusted watch. "I should freshen up before this evening's entertainment. Thank you again, Captain."

As the woman walked away, Manny turned to Tessa with a warm smile that faltered when he saw her expression.

"I am happy to see you," he began. "How was Capri?"

"Beautiful," Tessa replied flatly. "Almost as impressive as watching you arrange dates between wealthy women and known predators."

Manny's smile disappeared. "Excuse me?"

"Patrick Desmond?" Tessa crossed her arms. "The man who's been working his way through single women on this ship like it's his personal hunting ground?"

"Tessa, I think you've misunderstood."

"Have I? Because it sounded very clear to me that you're facilitating these 'arrangements'." Her voice sharpened. "Do you get a commission? Or is it just the satisfaction of helping men prey on vulnerable women?"

Manny's eyes darkened. "That's not what's happening here."

"Then please, enlighten me." Tessa gestured expansively. "Explain how the captain of this ship is personally arranging dinner dates between lotharios and wealthy widows."

"I know all my guests, Tessa. I look after them."

"By feeding them to sharks?" She shook her head in disgust. "I thought better of you, Manny. I really did."

A muscle twitched in his jaw. "You don't have all the facts."

"I have enough." Tessa took a step back. "To think I almost…" She stopped herself. "Enjoy your evening, Captain."

She turned on her heel and walked away, ignoring him when he called after her. Her cheeks burned with anger and embarrassment. The man she'd been daydreaming about, planning private tours with, was nothing more than an enabler for con men targeting women like her friends… like her.

As she punched the elevator button, she wondered what other illusions would shatter before this cruise ended.

Chapter 6

The Luna di Mare Lounge shimmered with soft lighting as evening descended. Tessa, Julia, Seren, and Kelly claimed a corner banquette offering both privacy and a sweeping view of the darkening Mediterranean. Four martini glasses glistened on the polished table between them, though Tessa's remained virtually untouched.

"I still can't believe it," Tessa said, her voice tight with controlled anger. "The captain of this ship, this luxury cruise line, actively arranges 'companions' for wealthy women. It's practically procuring."

Julia's brow furrowed. "Are you absolutely certain that's what was happening? Perhaps there's an innocent explanation."

"What innocent explanation could there possibly be for 'I'll arrange for you to have dinner with Patrick Desmond'?" Tessa mimicked the captain's accent with biting precision.

Seren took a thoughtful sip of her martini. "Even so, darling, perhaps the captain is simply accommodating guests' requests. If that woman asked to meet Patrick…"

"Then why did he say there are three companions on board?" Tessa countered. "Like he's keeping inventory."

Kelly looked up from her phone momentarily. "People ask cruise staff to make introductions all the time, Mom. It doesn't mean the captain is running some kind of gigolo ring."

"I saw the way Patrick operates with my own eyes," Tessa insisted. "And Richard Collier, too. These men target vulnerable women, and apparently with the captain's blessing."

Julia reached across the table to cover Tessa's hand with her own. "I understand why you're upset, especially given your… feelings for Manny. But it does seem out of character for him."

"I barely know the man," Tessa retorted, though the flush creeping up her neck betrayed her. "And clearly what I thought I knew was wrong."

Julia drew Kelly's attention from her phone. "What about your new friend, Kelly? Could Liam be part of this supposed ring, too?"

"I've been wondering the same thing," Tessa admitted. "He appeared very suddenly, very interested in you, a successful, single woman."

Kelly's head snapped up fully, her eyes flashing. "That's ridiculous. Liam is a legitimate investment banker. We've talked shop for hours, details you can't fake."

"Con men are excellent researchers," Tessa countered. "They learn just enough to seem credible."

"You're wrong about him," Kelly said firmly. "And probably wrong about the captain too."

Tessa opened her mouth to argue further when Kelly suddenly gasped, her eyes widening at something on her phone screen.

"Oh my God."

"What is it?" Julia leaned forward.

Kelly turned her phone around, revealing a news article with a grainy photograph. "I was doing a search about companions-for-hire on cruises, just to prove Mom wrong, and found this instead."

The three women leaned in to examine the screen. The headline read: "FBI Seeks Man Accused of Conning Miami Widow He Met on Luxury Cruise." Below it was a surveillance photo showing a man escorting an elderly woman through what appeared to be a cruise terminal.

"That's Patrick Desmond," Seren whispered, pointing at the screen. "Same man, different name maybe, but definitely him."

Tessa felt a chill run through her. "Read it."

Kelly scrolled through the article, summarizing as she went. "Miami widow, 74… met on a transatlantic cruise… introduced by the captain… posed as an international businessman… gained her trust during the voyage… convinced her to invest in fake overseas opportunities… drained her retirement savings…"

Julia's expression darkened. "It says he may be using forged documents and multiple aliases."

"And he's known to travel between Florida, New York, and Europe," Kelly added, looking up with concern etching her features.

Tessa's vindication was tempered by genuine alarm. "So, Patrick Desmond is a wanted criminal… one the FBI is actively searching for… and he's on this ship targeting women. With the captain's assistance."

"We don't know that part for certain," Julia cautioned.

"But we do know Patrick is dangerous," Seren said, her usual lightheartedness replaced by sober concern. "And there are at least two other men operating similarly on this cruise."

The four women exchanged troubled glances as the implications sank in.

"What do we do?" Kelly asked, suddenly looking less certain about her defense of Liam. "Should we tell security? Go directly to the captain?"

"The captain already knows," Tessa said bitterly. "He's part of it."

"We don't have proof of that," Julia reminded her. "And we need to be careful. If these men are truly dangerous…"

"We could be putting ourselves at risk by confronting them," Seren finished, unusually solemn.

"Or putting other women at risk by doing nothing," Tessa countered.

Kelly set her phone down, the FBI article still displayed. "We need to tell someone. Security, at minimum. They need to know they have a wanted criminal on board."

Tessa drew a deep breath, her legal training finally overtaking her emotional reaction. Her fingers drummed against the table as her analytical mind clicked into familiar patterns.

"We need to approach this methodically," she said, her voice steadying. "As an attorney, I've seen vigilante efforts destroy legitimate investigations. Our first step should be notifying ship security, discreetly. We provide them with the information we have, including the FBI article, and let them handle it from there."

Julia nodded in agreement. "That makes perfect sense."

* * *

Julia and Tessa approached the sleek Guest Services desk on Deck 5, requesting a private conversation with security. After a brief wait, they were escorted to a small office tucked behind the main reception area. The Chief Security Officer, a broad-shouldered man with a neatly trimmed beard and the watchful eyes of someone who missed very little, rose to greet them.

"Mrs. Monroe, Mrs. Benton," he said, extending his hand. "I'm Nikolai Petrov, head of security. How can I assist you this evening?"

Julia took the lead, explaining their discovery as concisely as possible. She showed him the FBI article on her phone, pointing out the striking resemblance between the man in the photo and Patrick Desmond.

"We believe this man is currently aboard the Aurelia, possibly operating under the name 'Patrick Desmond,'" she concluded. "And we have reason to believe he may be targeting wealthy female passengers, specifically Vivian Rothschild."

Petrov studied the article and photo carefully, his expression revealing nothing.

"I appreciate you bringing this to my attention," he said finally, handing the phone back to Julia. "This does appear to resemble Mr. Desmond."

"Then you'll detain him?" Tessa asked, leaning forward. "Contact the authorities?"

Petrov's response was measured. "Unfortunately, the situation is not that straightforward. While I agree there is a resemblance, I have no jurisdiction to intervene unless a passenger commits an offense aboard this vessel."

"But this man is wanted by the FBI," Julia protested.

"For alleged crimes committed in the United States," Petrov clarified. "We're currently in international waters, heading toward Italian territory. Without direct evidence of criminal activity aboard this ship, or an international warrant presented through proper channels, my hands are tied."

Tessa's demeanor hardened. "So, you're saying a known con man can just sail around targeting women, and you'll do nothing?"

"I'm saying I must operate within maritime law and the protocols of this cruise line," Petrov replied calmly. "I will, however, increase surveillance on this individual and contact our legal department regarding next steps."

He leaned forward, his tone becoming more confidential. "In the meantime, I must ask that you and your friends keep this information to yourselves and avoid direct contact with Mr. Desmond or either of the other gentlemen you mentioned. If he is who you suspect, confronting him could potentially create a situation none of us wants."

* * *

Petrov strode through the ship's corridors with purpose, his face set in stern lines. Crew members stepped aside at his approach, recognizing the urgency in his gait. He reached the bridge and rapped sharply on the door before entering.

Captain Delgado looked up from the navigation console, his silver hair catching the blue glow of the instruments. "Chief? What brings you here at this hour?"

"Captain, we have a situation." Petrov crossed to where Manny stood and lowered his voice. "Mrs. Monroe and Mrs. Benton came to security with concerns about Patrick Desmond. They've identified him from an FBI article as a suspected con man who's targeted wealthy women on cruise ships."

Manny's expression darkened. His fingers tightened imperceptibly around the edge of the console. "Are they certain?"

"It is clearly him," Petrov confirmed. "They showed me the article. I advised them to keep the information to themselves and avoid contact with the suspect."

Manny turned away, facing the expansive windows overlooking the darkened Mediterranean. The lights from distant fishing vessels dotted the horizon like earthbound stars. He'd known Tessa had strong opinions about men who entertained women on cruise ships. Her disgust had been evident during their dinner when she'd questioned Richard Collier. And now this.

"Did they mention their suspicions about my… involvement?" Manny asked, his Italian accent thickening slightly.

Petrov shook his head. "Not directly to me. But Mrs. Monroe seemed particularly disturbed by the whole situation."

Manny sighed heavily. He'd hoped to shield Tessa from his operation, at least until he could explain properly. Now that seemed increasingly unlikely.

"Our undercover team is still monitoring all three subjects?" Manny asked.

"Yes, Captain. Desmond, Collier, and Marquez remain under constant surveillance. They've made contact with several female passengers, but we've observed no criminal activity yet."

"And our FBI guests have everything they need?"

"They have remained very discreet, and Mrs. Rothschild is under constant surveillance."

"Good." Manny rubbed his jaw thoughtfully. "They need evidence, not just suspicion, before they can act. These men are clever; they know exactly how far they can push without technically breaking laws."

"Shall I increase security around Mrs. Monroe and her companions?" Petrov asked.

"No… that might alert our targets." Manny straightened his uniform jacket. "Just maintain current protocols and report any developments directly to me, no matter the hour."

"Understood, Captain."

"And Nikolai…" Manny's voice stopped the security chief at the door. "Thank you for handling this discreetly."

As Petrov departed, Manny turned back to the sea, his mind churning with complications. The operation was stressful enough without Tessa's involvement. Now he faced not only helping the FBI capture a sophisticated criminal but also the possible loss of something he'd come to value more than he'd expected.

* * *

The women reconvened at Oceano, the ship's seafood restaurant, settling into a secluded corner table with the Mediterranean night spread beyond floor-to-ceiling windows. Their faces reflected in the dark glass as servers glided between tables with platters of grilled fish and shellfish towers.

"Security has no jurisdiction unless a crime is committed on the ship," Julia summarized, breaking apart a crusty roll. "We're essentially watching a crime unfold in slow motion."

Tessa pushed her sea bass around her plate. "And the captain is facilitating it. I still can't believe it."

"We don't know that for certain," Seren pointed out, gesturing with her wine glass. "Perhaps he's merely following some misguided customer service directive: 'make all guests happy', even the criminals."

"Either way," Kelly interjected, "we've done what we can. We've alerted security. The rest is beyond our control."

Tessa's fork clattered against her plate. "I'm canceling my plans with Manny for Porto Cervo. I can't possibly spend an entire day with him now."

"That might be hasty," Julia said carefully. "Think about it, Tess. If the captain is innocent of any wrongdoing, you're throwing away something potentially wonderful based on circumstantial evidence."

"And if he is involved?" Tessa challenged.

"Then you might learn something valuable," Julia replied. "You're an attorney, after all. If anyone can subtly extract information without raising suspicions, it's you."

Seren nodded enthusiastically. "Julia's right. Besides, you'll be in public places. It's not as though he's luring you to some deserted cove."

"I don't know…" Tessa began.

"Mom, you were excited about that excursion," Kelly added. "Don't let suspicion ruin what could be a perfectly wonderful day."

Tessa stared out at the darkness, weighing their advice against her disappointment. "Fine. I'll go. But I'll be watching him carefully."

"That's our girl," Seren said with a wink. "Always did love a good cross-examination."

Their conversation was interrupted by the chime of Kelly's phone. She glanced at the screen, and her face transformed, eyes brightening, lips curving into an unguarded smile.

"Excuse me," she said, already rising. "I need to take this."

"Everything alright?" Tessa asked.

"Just a friend from San Francisco," Kelly replied, fingers already moving to accept the call. "Won't be long."

As Kelly moved toward a quieter corner of the restaurant, Tessa watched her daughter's body language: the slight bounce in her step, the way she tucked her hair behind her ear before answering.

"That didn't look like 'just a friend' to me," Seren observed, following Tessa's gaze.

"No," Tessa agreed, feeling a familiar maternal twinge of being kept at arm's length. "It certainly didn't."

Chapter 7

The morning sun painted Rome in golden hues as their private car wound through the ancient streets from Civitavecchia toward Aventine Hill. Tessa, Julia, Seren, and Kelly gazed out the windows, each lost in her own thoughts about the previous night's discoveries, yet determined to enjoy their day in the Eternal City.

"I've been looking forward to this since we booked the cruise," Julia said, notebook already in hand. "There's something about Rome that feels like coming home, even if you've never been here before."

Their guide, Francesca, a petite woman with animated gestures and impeccable English, led them up the winding paths of Aventine Hill. The scent of orange blossoms perfumed the air as they entered the Giardino degli Aranci.

"The Orange Garden," Francesca translated, sweeping her arm toward the grove. "One of Rome's best-kept secrets."

The women wandered among the trees, pausing at a terrace that offered a breathtaking panorama of the city. St. Peter's dome rose majestically in the distance, commanding the skyline.

"My goodness," Seren breathed, lifting her face to the sun. "I believe I was a Roman Goddess in a former life."

Julia snapped photos while scribbling notes, her writer's mind clearly cataloging sensory details for future use. Tessa stood slightly apart, her thoughts still tangled with concerns about Manny, until Kelly nudged her.

"Mom, you're in Rome. Captain drama can wait until tomorrow."

Tessa smiled reluctantly. "You're right. This view is too spectacular to waste."

Their next stop was the famed keyhole of the Knights of Malta. One by one, they took turns peering through the tiny aperture, each gasping at the perfectly framed view of St. Peter's dome through a tunnel of manicured hedges.

"It's like looking through time," Julia murmured, stepping back. "A secret portal to another world."

While making their way down to the Tiber to venture into Trastevere, Kelly abruptly halted, her gaze drawn to a recognizable silhouette walking by himself near the water's edge.

"Is that… Liam?" she asked, squinting against the sun.

The others followed her gaze. There was no mistaking his tall frame and confident stride as he paused to take in the view of the river.

"You should say hello," Seren suggested with a mischievous gleam.

Kelly hesitated. "We were supposed to have ladies' day."

"Go on," Tessa encouraged, her suspicions about Liam momentarily set aside in the magic of Rome. "No one should experience Rome alone."

Kelly jogged ahead, calling Liam's name. The others watched as he turned, his face lighting with recognition. After a brief exchange, Kelly waved the group over.

"Would you mind if Liam joined us?" she asked. "He was planning to explore Trastevere too."

"The more the merrier," Seren declared before anyone could object.

Julia nudged Kelly playfully as they crossed the Ponte Cestio into Trastevere. "Just friends, you said last night?"

Kelly rolled her eyes. "Yes, just friends. You can have male friends without romantic entanglements, you know."

"Of course," Tessa agreed with exaggerated innocence. "Especially ones who look at you the way he does."

"Mom!" Kelly protested, though her cheeks colored slightly.

Liam, walking ahead with Francesca and discussing the history of the neighborhood, remained oblivious to their teasing.

Trastevere welcomed them with its labyrinth of cobblestone streets and buildings draped in ivy and flowering plants. Laundry strung between windows added splashes of color against the weathered facades.

"This is where real Romans live," Liam commented, glancing up at the architectural details. "My father used to bring me here when I was a boy. He had business in Rome frequently."

"You've been here before?" Seren asked.

Liam nodded. "Many times. Though it's been years since my last visit."

As they wandered deeper into the quarter, Liam proved surprisingly knowledgeable, pointing out hidden courtyards and architectural details that even Francesca hadn't mentioned.

"The Basilica of Santa Cecilia is just around this corner," he said, guiding them through a narrow passage. "It's often overlooked, but the crypt is fascinating."

Inside the church, Julia marveled at the ancient mosaics while Seren closed her eyes in silent meditation. Kelly and Liam stood before the haunting sculpture of the martyred saint, their heads bent close in whispered conversation.

Tessa watched them from a distance, still uncertain about Liam's intentions but struck by how natural they looked together.

When they emerged back into the sunlight, Liam checked his watch. "It's nearly lunchtime. If you're hungry, I know a place the tourists haven't discovered yet."

"Our itinerary mentions Osteria da Enzo," Julia said, consulting her notes.

Liam's face brightened. "Excellent choice! It's exactly where I was going to suggest. The cacio e pepe is transcendent."

They navigated the maze-like streets toward the restaurant, with Liam occasionally pointing out hidden details and sharing anecdotes about Roman history, and the initial awkwardness of his joining them melted away. By the time they arrived at the small, unassuming osteria tucked in a quiet piazza, he felt like a natural part of their group.

"I've been suspicious for nothing," Tessa thought as they settled at a table beneath a trellis of grape vines. The aroma of garlic and basil filled the air, and nearby, local Romans gestured animatedly over plates of pasta. Liam fit seamlessly into their dynamic, respectful of their friendship, while adding his own perspective.

When the wine was poured and bread baskets passed, Tessa caught Kelly's eye across the table. Her daughter smiled, not the guarded smile she often wore in her mother's presence, but something more relaxed and genuine. Whatever Liam was to Kelly, friend, colleague, or possibly something more, he clearly brought out something good in her.

For now, in the golden Roman afternoon, that was enough.

* * *

The warm sun bathed the courtyard of Osteria da Enzo as platters of traditional Roman dishes appeared on their table, cacio e pepe with perfectly al dente pasta, artichokes prepared in the local style, and carafes of crisp white wine that caught the light like liquid gold.

"This is sublime," Julia sighed after her first bite of pasta. "How did you know about this place, Liam?"

Liam twirled pasta around his fork with practiced ease. "My father brought me here years ago. Some places in Rome change with every tourist season, but the truly special ones remain exactly as you remember them."

"You mentioned you were traveling alone," Seren said, refilling everyone's wine glasses. "Was that the plan all along?"

A shadow of something, disappointment perhaps, crossed Liam's face. "Actually, my friend Daniel was supposed to join me. We've been planning this cruise for months, but his mother fell ill just days before departure." He shrugged. "He insisted I go anyway. The tickets were non-refundable, and honestly, I needed the break from work."

"That was bad timing," Tessa said, studying him with slightly less suspicion than before.

"It worked out, though, didn't it?" Kelly interjected. "You get to spend part of your trip with four wonderful women."

Liam's expression brightened. "Absolutely. Meeting all of you has been the unexpected highlight of this journey."

As they lingered over dessert, a shared selection of tiramisu and panna cotta, Francesca reminded them of their afternoon schedule along the Appian Way. The ancient Roman road awaited, with its archaeological treasures and the mysterious catacombs beneath the surface.

The afternoon sun cast long shadows as they walked along the historic Via Appia Antica, their footsteps echoing on the same massive stone slabs that had supported Roman legions two millennia earlier. Cypress trees lined the route, standing like sentinels against the cloudless blue sky.

While Francesca explained the engineering marvel of the road's construction to Julia and Tessa, Kelly had fallen several paces behind, her attention divided between the ancient surroundings and her smartphone. Her thumbs moved rapidly across the screen, her expression alternating between concentration and amusement.

"Your daughter seems quite attached to that phone," Liam commented to Tessa as they paused to examine a crumbling mausoleum.

Tessa sighed. "Some things never change. She's always been like that, present in body, elsewhere in mind."

"The curse of our generation," Liam admitted. "Though I've been trying to disconnect more during this trip."

Ahead of them, Seren and Julia were engrossed in Francesca's explanation of the aqueduct system visible in the distance. Behind them, Kelly positioned herself beside a particularly picturesque section of the ancient road, angled her phone, and snapped a selfie with Liam caught in the background.

"Come join me," she called to him. "Let's get one together."

Liam obliged, standing beside her as she took another photo, both smiling against the backdrop of antiquity. Kelly immediately began typing.

"Sending that to someone special?" Tessa asked, catching up to them.

"Just Briana back in San Francisco," Kelly replied casually. "I promised I would send photos."

As the group continued toward the entrance to the catacombs, Kelly and Liam lingered behind, their heads bent in conversation. Seren, who had paused to admire a cluster of wildflowers growing between the ancient stones, couldn't help overhearing their exchange.

"Have you mentioned anything to your mother yet?" Liam asked, his voice low but clear in the quiet countryside.

Kelly shook her head. "Not with everything else going on—the lotharios, her suspicions about the captain. It hasn't seemed like the right time."

"Don't wait too long," Liam advised gently. "The longer you put it off, the harder it becomes. Trust me on this."

Kelly sighed. "I know. I just need to find the right moment."

Their conversation halted as they realized Seren was within earshot. Kelly quickly changed the subject to the architecture of the catacombs they were about to explore.

Seren pretended not to have heard, but filed the exchange away for later consideration. Whatever Kelly was keeping from Tessa seemed significant enough to weigh on her.

The underground chambers of the catacombs provided a cool respite from the afternoon heat; their narrow passages were lined with ancient burial niches and early Christian symbols. In the dim lighting, the modern world felt distant, time compressed into the silent testimony of those who had walked these paths centuries before.

As their guide led them through the labyrinthine network, Julia scribbled notes furiously, her writer's imagination clearly sparked by the atmospheric setting. Tessa found herself deeply moved by the humble faith represented in the simple carvings, while Seren closed her eyes occasionally, as if communing with the spirits that lingered in the stone.

By the time they emerged back into the sunlight, a sense of contented exhaustion had settled over the group. The drive back to Civitavecchia passed in comfortable conversation, each of them processing the day's experiences in their own way.

As they disembarked from their tour van, Kelly linked her arm through Tessa's. "Thanks for letting Liam join us today."

Tessa squeezed her daughter's hand. "He was a wonderful addition. Maybe I've been too suspicious lately."

"Maybe," Kelly agreed with a soft smile. "Sometimes people just want connection, nothing sinister about that."

* * *

After returning to the ship, Tessa retreated to her suite to freshen up for dinner. Despite her lingering doubts about the captain, she'd agreed to meet him for cocktails afterward. He'd explained he needed to be on the bridge during sail away, but would join her at the Celestial Lounge once they were underway.

As she applied a touch of lipstick, she caught her own gaze in the mirror. "You're a grown woman, Tessa," she muttered to her reflection. "Just hear him out."

Dinner with Julia, Seren, and Kelly was pleasant if somewhat distracted. Kelly seemed particularly preoccupied, checking her phone beneath the table when she thought no one was looking. Julia and Seren exchanged knowing glances but said nothing.

"You're really going through with meeting the captain?" Julia asked as they finished dessert.

Tessa nodded. "I need to know the truth. And like you said, maybe there's an explanation."

"Just keep your attorney's hat firmly in place," Seren advised, raising her coffee cup in a mock toast.

After bidding the others goodnight, Tessa made her way toward the Celestial Lounge. The ship had already pulled away from Civitavecchia, and the gentle motion beneath her feet felt steadying somehow.

As she approached the lounge entrance, a familiar sound caught her attention: the lyrical notes of a Chopin nocturne floating from the adjacent piano bar. Glancing inside, she spotted Vivian Rothschild seated intimately close to Patrick Desmond, their heads bent together as they enjoyed the pianist's performance. Patrick's hand rested comfortably on Vivian's jeweled fingers, and the elderly woman's expression was animated, almost girlish. They looked for all the world like longtime companions rather than predator and prey.

Tessa hesitated, momentarily thrown by the genuine-seeming connection between them. Before she could process what she was seeing, a familiar accented voice spoke behind her.

"They make an interesting pair, no?"

She turned to find Captain Delgado standing there, resplendent in his formal whites.

"I thought we were meeting in the Celestial Lounge," she said, more stiffly than she'd intended.

"We are. I saw you from across the atrium and thought I would escort you." He offered his arm with old-world courtesy.

The Celestial Lounge was quieter, its panoramic windows showcasing the starlit Mediterranean. Once they were seated with drinks, a gin and tonic for her, sparkling water for him, Manny leaned forward.

"I understand Julia and Seren spoke with our Chief Security Officer about their concerns regarding Mr. Desmond."

Tessa's eyebrows rose. "News travels fast."

"On a ship, always." His expression grew serious. "Tessa, I want to assure you that I am not involved with any 'lothario gang,' as you call it. My only concern is the safety and enjoyment of my passengers."

"Then why were you arranging for Vivian to meet Patrick?"

Manny sighed. "It is… complicated. But I ask you to trust me, and to allow my security team to do their job. There are situations that require delicate handling."

"That's not much of an explanation," Tessa challenged.

"No, it is not," he admitted. "But it is all I can offer at the moment." His eyes held hers. "I have never lied to you, Tessa. I would not begin now."

She studied him, years of courtroom experience helping her weigh his sincerity. Something in his steady gaze made her want to believe him.

"Fine," she said finally. "I'll trust you… tentatively."

Relief softened his features. "Grazie. That is all I ask." He lifted his water glass. "To give people the benefit of the doubt."

Tessa clinked her glass against his, a small smile tugging at her lips despite her reservations. "Are we still on for tomorrow? Porto Cervo?"

"Absolutely," Manny replied, his expression brightening. "I will meet you at the tender platform at nine. The Costa Smeralda is spectacular; I promise you will not be disappointed."

Their conversation shifted to lighter topics, but Tessa couldn't shake her suspicions. Perhaps it was just her legal instincts on overdrive, or perhaps Manny was a skilled con artist just like the other men.

Chapter 8

Morning arrived with a brilliance that only the Mediterranean could deliver. Tessa woke earlier than necessary, spending extra time selecting her outfit, a flowing sundress in azure blue that matched the sea, paired with comfortable walking sandals and a wide-brimmed hat. She also applied her makeup with unusual care; well, that was between her and her mirror.

Captain Delgado waited at the tender platform precisely at nine, dressed in crisp linen pants and a white button-down shirt with the sleeves rolled to his elbows. Without his uniform, he appeared more approachable yet somehow no less commanding. Several female passengers cast appreciative glances his way, which he either didn't notice or politely ignored.

"You look beautiful," he said simply when Tessa approached.

"You clean up nicely yourself, Captain," she replied with a smile that belied the nervous flutter in her chest.

"Manny, please. Today I am not the captain, just a man showing a lovely woman one of my favorite places."

The tender bounced across the sparkling waters toward the harbor of Porto Cervo. Once ashore, Manny led her to a vintage Alfa Romeo convertible waiting in a private parking area.

"Borrowed from an old friend," he explained, opening the passenger door with a flourish.

They set off along the coastal road, the wind tousling Tessa's carefully arranged hair as Manny navigated the curves with confident ease. The

Costa Smeralda lived up to its name, emerald waters lapped against rocky shores while lush Mediterranean vegetation clung to the hillsides.

"How did you discover this place?" Tessa asked as they pulled over at a panoramic overlook. Below them, the Maddalena Archipelago stretched across the horizon like jewels scattered on blue velvet.

"My father was a fisherman from Naples," Manny replied, leaning against the car's hood. "When I was twelve, he took a contract with a wealthy family who summered here. I spent three months exploring every cove and hillside while he worked."

Tessa studied his profile against the brilliant sky. "Is that when you fell in love with the sea?"

"Perhaps." His smile held a touch of nostalgia. "Or perhaps it was always in my blood. My mother said I was born during a thunderstorm, with the sound of waves as my first lullaby."

They drove further inland, the conversation flowing easily between them. Manny spoke of his early years in the merchant marine, his gradual rise to cruise ship captain. Tessa shared stories of her law school days, her struggle to balance motherhood and career.

Neither mentioned Patrick Desmond nor the other men aboard the ship. Today was for them alone.

By midday, they arrived at a stone farmhouse nestled among vineyards and olive groves. An elderly woman with a weathered face and bright eyes greeted Manny with enthusiastic kisses on both cheeks, speaking rapid Italian that made him laugh.

"Maria says we are too thin and must eat everything she has prepared," he translated for Tessa. "I should warn you, refusing seconds is considered an insult."

The agriturismo's dining room was cool and rustic, with wooden beams overhead and stone floors beneath. They were seated at a table near an open window where the scent of rosemary and sage drifted in on the breeze.

Course after course appeared: handmade malloreddus pasta with sausage and tomato, suckling pig roasted with myrtle, artichokes prepared with mint, and a parade of local cheeses. A robust Cannonau wine complemented the meal, its earthy notes perfect against the rich flavors.

"This is incredible," Tessa sighed, accepting another spoonful of seadas—fried pastry filled with cheese and drizzled with honey.

Manny watched her enjoyment with evident pleasure. "Food tastes better when shared with good company, no?"

His fingers brushed against hers as he refilled her wine glass, and Tessa felt that touch all the way to her core.

* * *

After lunch, they wound deeper into the hills, the Alfa Romeo purring around curves that revealed increasingly spectacular views. The sun hung high overhead, turning the vineyards into a patchwork of gold and green.

"Our next stop is special," Manny said, turning onto a narrow dirt road. "Giovanni makes only three hundred bottles per year. He sells to no stores, no distributors. You must come to him."

They pulled up to a stone cottage with a small sign: "Vini Corsaro." A bearded man in his fifties emerged, arms outstretched.

"Manuel! Finalmente!" He clasped Manny in a bear hug before turning curious eyes to Tessa.

"Giovanni, this is Tessa. Tessa, my old friend Giovanni, who makes wine like his ancestors did two centuries ago."

Giovanni led them through a modest cellar where oak barrels rested in cool darkness. The tour ended at a weathered wooden table beneath a pergola dripping with wisteria. Three bottles awaited them, along with a wooden board of crusty bread, olive oil, and a soft cheese.

"First, the Vermentino," Giovanni announced, pouring a pale golden liquid into their glasses. "From vines that taste of the sea breeze."

As they sampled each wine, Giovanni shared stories of harvests past, of midnight grape-picking under full moons, of fermentation mysteries handed down through generations. Eventually, he excused himself to tend to the vines, leaving them alone.

Manny poured the last drops of Cannonau into Tessa's glass. "Tell me something I don't know about you."

Tessa traced the rim of her glass with one finger. "That's a dangzrous invitation."

"I'll risk it."

She took a breath, the wine having loosened the locks on thoughts she usually kept private. "My marriage was a business arrangement that lasted thirty-eight years. I thought it was successful until I discovered James had been having affairs for most of it."

Manny's expression darkened. "I'm sorry."

"Don't be. I wasn't blameless. I invested everything in my career and Kelly." She looked up at him. "What about you? No wife waiting in some port?"

"No." Manny gazed out over the vineyards. "The sea is a jealous mistress. Many women find the romance of a captain appealing until they realize I am gone more than I am home."

"Yet you must have opportunities. All those lonely women on cruises…" Tessa let the implication hang between them.

Manny's eyes met hers, sharp and knowing. "You wonder if I am like those men you suspect? If I charm women for… what? Money? Entertainment?"

Tessa felt heat rise to her face. "I didn't say that."

"You didn't need to." His voice held no anger, only a quiet certainty. "I have never pursued a passenger, Tessa. Not in twenty-three years at sea."

"Until me?"

"Until you." He reached across the table, his fingers tracing the back of her hand. "Some things are worth breaking rules for."

The intensity in his gaze made her look away. "And what happens when the cruise ends?"

"That depends on what you want to happen."

She surprised herself with her honesty. "I don't know what I want anymore. For decades, I knew exactly—partner at the firm, college fund for Kelly, the house in Bethesda. Now…"

"Now you are free to choose again."

"I've been thinking about traveling. Really traveling, not just two-week vacations between cases. There are places I've read about my whole life but never seen."

Manny's smile deepened the creases around his eyes. "The world is wide and beautiful. Where would you begin?"

"Maybe the Greek islands. Or Morocco. Or Japan during cherry blossom season." Excitement colored her voice.

"All excellent choices."

As they left the winery, the late afternoon light cast long shadows across the landscape. Manny drove more slowly now, in no hurry to end their day. They stopped at a secluded beach where the Tyrrhenian Sea lapped gently against pink-tinged sand.

Walking barefoot along the water's edge, Tessa felt his hand reach for hers. She hesitated only briefly before twining her fingers with his, the sensation both foreign and achingly familiar.

* * *

The evening cast a velvet glow across the Luna di Mare Lounge as Kelly and Liam occupied a corner table, positioned with a perfect view of both the entrance and the intimate alcove where Vivian Rothschild sat in hushed conversation with Patrick Desmond. The soft jazz from the trio on stage provided just enough cover for their words to remain private, but not enough to completely mask fragments that drifted toward Kelly's attentive ears.

"Mom should be here any minute," Kelly said, checking her watch. "She texted that they're heading back to the ship now."

Liam nodded, swirling the amber liquid in his glass. "Kelly, we need to talk about…"

"I know, I know." She sighed, running a finger along the rim of her wine glass. "I should tell her. But the timing feels wrong with everything that's happening."

"There's never a perfect time," Liam said gently. "But secrets between mothers and daughters have a way of creating distance. Trust me on this."

Kelly's eyes drifted to Vivian and Patrick's table. The older woman looked completely captivated, leaning forward with sparkling eyes as Patrick spoke with animated gestures.

"What are you so afraid of?" Liam pressed. "Your mother seems open-minded, supportive."

"It's not that I think she'll reject me," Kelly admitted. "It's more like… I've hidden this part of myself for so long, it's become this… enormous thing between us. What if she's hurt that I didn't trust her sooner?"

Liam reached across the table to squeeze her hand. "She'll understand. Parents usually do."

Their conversation halted abruptly as Patrick's voice rose momentarily above the music. "… revolutionary AI platform that's poised to transform financial markets," he was saying, leaning closer to Vivian.

"Normally I wouldn't share this opportunity with someone I've just met, but there's something special about you, Vivian."

Vivian chuckled, a sound rich with worldly experience. "You flatter an old woman, Patrick."

"Not flattery when it's true." Patrick's voice dropped again, but Kelly and Liam strained to hear. "EvoGenAI has already secured first-round funding, but they're offering a limited private investment opportunity before their Series B. Double, perhaps triple returns within eighteen months."

Kelly and Liam exchanged alarmed glances.

"EvoGenAI?" Liam whispered. "I've never heard of them."

"Me neither," Kelly murmured, "and I vet AI startups for a living."

They watched as Patrick slid what appeared to be a business card across the table. Vivian examined it with practiced nonchalance before tucking it into her evening bag.

"Let me think about it," they heard her say. "Two hundred fifty thousand is a significant sum, even for me."

Patrick nodded magnanimously. "Of course. The opportunity closes in three days, but there's no pressure."

Kelly's pulse quickened. "We need to tell my mother. Now."

As if summoned by her words, Tessa appeared at the lounge entrance with Julia and Seren. Kelly waved them over urgently, already halfway out of her seat.

"You're not going to believe what we just heard," she said as soon as they were within earshot.

The three women settled around their table as Kelly and Liam quickly relayed Patrick's investment pitch.

"EvoGenAI?" Tessa frowned. "Never heard of it."

"Exactly," Kelly said. "And I'm in this space. If it were legitimate, I'd know about it."

"He's asking for a quarter of a million dollars," Liam added, "Claiming guaranteed returns within eighteen months."

Julia's eyes widened. "That poor woman."

"She doesn't seem particularly distressed," Seren observed, glancing discreetly toward Vivian, who was now laughing at something Patrick had said.

"Scammers like Patrick pick their targets carefully," Tessa said grimly. "Wealthy, confident women who don't see themselves as vulnerable are perfect marks."

"We have to stop him," Kelly insisted.

Tessa's face hardened with determination. "I'm seeing Manny later tonight. I'll tell him exactly what we heard. If he's truly not involved, he'll take action. If he brushes it off…" She let the implication hang in the air.

As they continued discussing strategies, Kelly noticed Liam watching her with a mix of concern and something else… pride, perhaps. She felt a surge of gratitude for his steady presence during this unexpected drama.

"What?" she asked when she caught his gaze.

"Just thinking you're exactly like your mother," he said quietly. "Fierce when someone needs protecting."

Kelly smiled, glancing at Tessa. "There are worse things to be."

Across the lounge, Patrick helped Vivian to her feet, his hand lingering on her elbow. The woman appeared completely at ease, her diamond bracelet catching the light as she gathered her purse.

"They're leaving," Seren whispered.

Tessa checked her watch. "I need to meet Manny in thirty minutes. I'll tell him everything: the investment scam, the FBI article, all of it. This has gone far enough."

"Be careful, Mom," Kelly cautioned, embracing Tessa. "And let us know what the captain says."

"I will," Tessa promised, squeezing her daughter's hand. "And Kelly? Whatever's on your mind, whatever you and Liam have been whispering about, you can tell me when you're ready."

Kelly's eyes widened slightly. "How did you…"

"I'm your mother," Tessa said simply with a small smile that held both wisdom and patience. "I notice things."

With that, she turned and walked away, leaving Kelly wondering if perhaps the perfect moment she'd been waiting for had just passed her by.

Chapter 9

As Tessa made her way toward the captain's quarters, a formally dressed junior officer in crisp whites intercepted her, touching her shoulder with respectful restraint.

"Mrs. Monroe?" His voice carried the practiced neutrality of delivering disappointing news. "Captain Delgado extends his deepest regrets. He's been detained due to a passenger emergency and won't be able to meet you as planned."

Tessa's heartbeat quickened. "Emergency? Is everyone alright?"

"The captain will contact you personally once the situation is resolved." The officer's face remained impassive, revealing nothing. "He asked me to tell you how truly sorry he is."

Tessa nodded, disappointment mingling with concern as the young man turned sharply and disappeared down a corridor marked "Crew Only." The information she needed to share about Patrick would have to wait.

Back in the Aurum Spiral Atrium, Tessa rejoined Julia, Seren, Kelly, and Liam, who had gathered near the grand staircase.

"That was fast," Julia remarked, studying Tessa's expression.

"I didn't see him. Apparently, there's some kind of emergency."

As if on cue, the ship's intercom crackled to life. The cruise director's voice, professionally calm yet tinged with apology, filled the space.

"Good evening, ladies and gentlemen. This is Elise Brennan, your cruise director. I'm informing you that our departure from Porto

Cervo will be delayed due to a passenger emergency. I want to assure you there is no cause for concern, and we anticipate arriving in Portofino tomorrow morning as scheduled. Thank you for your understanding, and please continue enjoying all the wonderful amenities the Aurelia has to offer."

The atrium hummed with speculative murmurs as passengers exchanged theories.

"A medical emergency, probably," an elderly gentleman nearby commented to his companion. "Someone's heart playing up after too much wine and sunshine."

"Or someone lost their passport," Seren suggested, but her light tone couldn't mask the concern in her eyes.

Liam leaned in, lowering his voice. "I've become friendly with one of the bartenders on Deck 9, Miguel. He might know something. Let me see what I can find out."

"You really think he'll tell you ship business?" Julia asked skeptically.

"You'd be surprised by what people share when they feel comfortable," Liam replied with an easy confidence. "Give me twenty minutes."

Tessa's eyes narrowed slightly. This was exactly the kind of charm and assurance Patrick displayed in the ability to extract information, to make connections quickly. Yet something about Liam felt genuine in a way Patrick did not.

"We'll wait in the Terraza del Sol," Tessa decided. "It's quieter there."

As Liam turned to leave, Kelly's phone buzzed insistently in her purse. She glanced at the screen, her expression instantly transforming from curiosity to irritation.

"Excuse me," she muttered, already stepping away. "I need to take this."

"Everything okay?" Tessa called after her.

Kelly waved dismissively without turning back. "Just work. Always work."

The three remaining women exchanged glances as they watched Kelly disappear around a corner, phone pressed tightly to her ear, her voice already rising in what sounded like a strained negotiation.

"Something's not right with her," Tessa said quietly. "And it's not just work."

"She's hiding something," Seren agreed, her usual exuberance tempered. "But we all have our timing for revelations."

Julia nodded thoughtfully. "The question is, what's happening on this ship that's serious enough to delay departure? And why do I have the strangest feeling it might connect to our lotharios?"

Tessa's gaze drifted toward the corridor where the junior officer had disappeared. "If it does involve Patrick or the others, then Manny's reaction will tell us everything we need to know about whose side he's really on."

The ship remained eerily still beneath their feet, its massive engines silent against the dark waters of Porto Cervo, as if the vessel itself were holding its breath, waiting for secrets to surface.

* * *

Nearly half an hour later, Liam slipped into a chair at the Terraza del Sol, his expression grim as he joined Tessa, Julia, and Seren. The women leaned forward instinctively, their cocktails forgotten. Kelly still hadn't returned from her mysterious phone call.

"Well?" Tessa prompted, her voice barely above a whisper despite the ambient music filling the lounge.

Liam glanced around before leaning in closer. "It's Gloria and Richard Collier. They didn't return to the ship."

"Both of them?" Julia's eyebrows rose.

"According to Miguel, they went ashore together this morning and never came back. No communication, nothing. Ship security is working with local authorities to locate them."

Seren frowned. "People miss the ship all the time. Usually, they just have to find their own way to the next port."

"Exactly," Liam agreed. "Miguel says it's highly unusual for the captain to delay departure for missing passengers. Normally, they're considered late and simply left behind."

The three women exchanged meaningful glances. Tessa's mind immediately constructed the darkest scenario.

"What if Richard did something to Gloria?" she said, her attorney's mind automatically building a case. "We know these men target wealthy women. What if she wouldn't give him money, or discovered his scheme?"

"That's quite a leap," Julia cautioned, ever the voice of reason. "They could have lost track of time or had transportation issues getting back."

"Without calling the ship?" Tessa challenged. "Everyone knows to contact the ship if you're running late."

"Perhaps they had too much wine with lunch," Seren suggested. "Or Gloria's having such a wonderful time, she decided to extend her stay."

"With a man we suspect is a predator," Tessa countered.

Liam cleared his throat. "Miguel mentioned something else interesting. Apparently, Richard Collier has been on this same itinerary three times in the past year."

Julia's expression sharpened. "That fits the pattern. Cruise ships are perfect hunting grounds for new faces each voyage, wealthy passengers looking for vacation romance."

"But why would the captain hold the ship for him?" Seren wondered aloud. "If Richard is part of this lothario ring, and Manny is somehow involved…"

"Then delaying departure could be about protecting their operation," Tessa finished, the knot in her stomach tightening. "Or maybe Gloria isn't the first woman to go missing after spending time with these men."

Julia placed her hand gently on Tessa's arm. "We need to be careful about jumping to conclusions. These are serious accusations without much evidence."

"Julia's right," Liam agreed. "The captain could have legitimate reasons for waiting. Perhaps Gloria is a high-value passenger, or there could be liability issues at play."

"Or maybe he genuinely cares about passengers' safety," Julia added, glancing pointedly at Tessa.

Tessa sighed, recognizing her tendency to build cases on limited facts as a professional habit hard to break. "You're right. We don't have enough information yet."

The subtle vibration of the ship beneath them suddenly ceased completely, the background hum of engines they'd grown accustomed to falling silent, making the vessel feel unnaturally still.

"They've powered down completely," Liam observed. "We're officially detained."

"For how long?" Seren asked.

Liam shrugged. "Miguel didn't know. But I'll check back with him later tonight. He comes on shift at the Aureate Cellar at eleven."

Tessa stared out at the twinkling lights of Porto Cervo; her reflection ghosted against the darkening Mediterranean beyond.

Two passengers missing, a ship delayed, and a captain who might be involved in something unsavory—the beautiful cruise she'd anticipated had transformed into something far more complex and potentially sinister.

"Where is Kelly?" she murmured, checking her watch. "She's been gone almost an hour."

As if conjured by her words, Kelly appeared at the entrance to the lounge, scanning the space until she spotted them. Her face was flushed, her movements agitated as she approached.

"Sorry about that," she said, sliding into the empty chair. "Work crisis."

"You missed the update," Seren told her. "Two passengers are missing, including our friend Richard Collier."

Kelly's eyes widened with genuine surprise. "Missing? What happened?"

As Liam repeated what he'd learned, Tessa studied her daughter's face, wondering why Kelly seemed so distracted.

* * *

"I heard there's a local folk ensemble performing in the Celestial Lounge in twenty minutes," Liam said, checking his watch.

"Sardinian music, supposedly quite remarkable—might take our minds off all this intrigue."

Kelly immediately shook her head. "I think I'd rather get some fresh air. Too much…" she waved her hand vaguely, "everything today." She turned to her mother. "Would you walk the deck with me? I could use the company."

Something in Kelly's tone caught Tessa's attention, a subtle vulnerability rarely displayed by her fiercely independent daughter.

"Of course," Tessa agreed, curious about what might prompt such a request.

Julia and Seren exchanged knowing glances.

"The show sounds lovely," Julia said, rising from her chair. "We'll join you, Liam."

"Perfect timing for us to catch up on old times," Seren added with a meaningful look at Tessa. The message was clear: they were giving mother and daughter some space.

The night air carried a hint of jasmine as Tessa and Kelly strolled along the near-empty promenade deck. The ship's lights cast a gentle glow against the surrounding darkness, while the distant shore of Porto Cervo twinkled like fallen stars.

"Remember when we used to take those weekend walks around Lake Merritt?" Kelly asked suddenly.

"When you were in college," Tessa smiled. "You'd come home from Berkeley, and we'd walk the entire loop, solving the world's problems."

"Or my problems, mostly," Kelly admitted. She took a deep breath. "Mom, there's something I've been meaning to tell you about my life in San Francisco."

Tessa felt her heart quicken. This was it… the secret Kelly had been dancing around.

"I've been seeing changes in your condo on our video calls," Tessa encouraged gently. "New art, different furniture arrangement."

Kelly nodded. "That's because of Briana. She moved in with me about eight months ago."

"Your friend from the yoga studio, The Breathing something?" Tessa recalled part of the name from previous conversations.

"The Breathing Tree, yes. But she's…" Kelly slowed her pace, gathering courage.

Tessa's attention suddenly snagged on a familiar figure by the railing ahead. Captain Delgado stood with his back to them, deep in conversation with Patrick Desmond. Without thinking, she gripped Kelly's arm and pulled her into the shadow of a lifeboat.

"Mom, what are you…"

"Shh," Tessa whispered, pointing. "It's Manny and Patrick."

Kelly frowned. "Are we seriously hiding and eavesdropping right now?"

"I need to know what they're saying," Tessa insisted, straining to hear.

The captain's voice carried on the night breeze. "… any idea what happened to them? When did you last see Richard and Gloria?"

Patrick shook his head. "We barely spoke today, Captain. He mentioned they were taking some private excursion to the Costa Smeralda. That's all I know."

"And you didn't notice anything unusual about his behavior?" Manny pressed.

"Look, we're not exactly friends," Patrick replied defensively. "We chat occasionally; that's it."

"If you hear anything… anything at all… you come directly to me," Manny instructed, his tone leaving no room for argument. "This situation is delicate."

"Yes, sir," Patrick nodded before both men walked away in opposite directions.

Kelly pulled back from their hiding spot, irritation clear on her face. "That was completely inappropriate."

"Don't you find it suspicious?" Tessa whispered, still processing what she'd heard. "Why is the captain interrogating Patrick specifically about Richard? There must be a connection between them."

"Or maybe he's asking everyone who might have information," Kelly countered. "You're letting your suspicions cloud your judgment."

Tessa reluctantly admitted Kelly might have a point. "I just want to understand what's happening."

"Mom." Kelly's voice turned serious as they resumed walking. "I was trying to tell you something important."

But the moment had shattered. Tessa could see Kelly withdrawing, the vulnerability replaced by frustration. After a minute of tense silence, Tessa tried a different approach.

"So, tell me about Liam. You two seem to get along well."

The question ignited something in Kelly. She stopped abruptly, turning to face her mother with uncharacteristic intensity.

"For God's sake, Mom! I have zero romantic interest in Liam!" Her voice rose before she caught herself, glancing around to ensure they were alone. "Liam is gay. He broke up with his partner, Daniel, right before this cruise. That's why he's traveling alone."

Tessa blinked in surprise. "I didn't…"

"And since we're on the subject," Kelly continued, words tumbling out in exasperation, "he's currently having a shipboard fling with Miguel. Yes, that Miguel, the bartender."

The revelation hit Tessa like a wave breaking over the bow. "Miguel and Liam? But how do you know…"

"Because Liam told me. Because we're friends. Because…" Kelly threw up her hands in frustration. "Because I understand him, Mom. I understand what it's like to have your family make assumptions about who you should be with."

Before Tessa could say anything, Kelly stormed off, leaving Tessa alone on the deck listening to the static of the intercom system.

"Ladies and gentlemen, this is your captain speaking. I'm pleased to inform you that we will be departing Porto Cervo shortly. Thank you for your patience."

Chapter 10

Tessa stood frozen on the deck, the captain's announcement barely registering as she watched Kelly disappear around the corner. Her daughter's final words echoed in her mind: *"I understand what it's like to have your family make assumptions about who you should be with."*

The implication hit her with sudden clarity. Kelly wasn't just defending Liam; she was talking about herself. The roommate, Briana. The mysterious phone calls. The reluctance to discuss relationships.

"Oh," Tessa whispered to the empty deck. How could I have missed it?

She hurried toward the elevators, her heart pounding. She needed to find Kelly to finish the conversation that had been interrupted, to make sure her daughter knew that nothing… absolutely nothing… would change her love for her.

As she rounded the corner toward the central atrium, Liam, Julia, and Seren emerged from the lounge, their faces brightening when they spotted her.

"Tessa!" Julia called. "There you are. We have news."

Tessa glanced anxiously past them toward the elevators. "Can it wait? I really need to…"

"They found Gloria and Richard," Seren interrupted, her voice brimming with relief.

This stopped Tessa short. "Found them? Where?"

"At the local hospital," Liam explained. "Gloria became violently ill during their excursion… some kind of severe food reaction. Richard took her to the emergency room."

"The captain just announced it to everyone in the lounge," Julia added.

"Apparently, Richard stayed behind to contact Gloria's family. He'll meet the ship in Portofino tomorrow."

"So no foul play?" Tessa asked, her suspicions momentarily diverting her from her mission.

"None whatsoever," Seren confirmed. "The doctor confirmed Gloria's condition and the timeline. The captain delayed departure until he had confirmation she was stable."

"That's… good," Tessa said distractedly, already moving toward the elevators again. "I'm sorry, but I really need to find Kelly right now."

"Is everything okay?" Julia's brow furrowed with concern.

"I think so… I hope so," Tessa called over her shoulder. "I'll explain later."

She had barely pressed the elevator button when a familiar accented voice called her name. Captain Delgado approached, his white uniform crisp despite the late hour, concern etched on his weathered face.

"Tessa, I was hoping to find you. We need to talk about what you overheard earlier…"

"Manny," she interrupted gently, "I'm sure we do, and I want to hear everything you have to say. But right now, I need to talk to my daughter."

His expression shifted from professional authority to personal concern. "Is Kelly alright? Has something happened?"

Tessa was touched by his genuine worry. "She's fine, physically. But we were in the middle of an important conversation when…" she gestured vaguely, "… when I got distracted. I need to finish that conversation."

"And this conversation is urgent?" he asked, studying her face.

"It's about her life, her happiness," Tessa said simply. "So yes, it's the most urgent thing in the world right now."

Understanding dawned in his eyes. He nodded and stepped back. "Family first, always."

"Thank you." She impulsively touched his arm. "I'm glad Gloria is okay, by the way. And I'm sorry for jumping to conclusions."

"We'll talk tomorrow," he promised. "Go find your daughter."

The elevator doors opened, and Tessa stepped inside, pressing the button for Deck 8, where Kelly's stateroom was located. As the doors closed, she caught a glimpse of Manny's expression: a mixture of respect and something warmer that made her chest tighten despite her current mission.

The ship's engines hummed beneath her feet as the Aurelia finally pulled away from Porto Cervo, heading toward their next destination. But Tessa's most important journey was the one she was about to take with her daughter, a journey of understanding that had been too long delayed.

                                 * * *

Tessa rapped on Kelly's stateroom door with more force than she intended. The gentle sway of the ship beneath her feet reminded her they were finally underway, but her mind was focused entirely on what waited behind that door.

The door swung open to reveal Kelly, her eyes slightly red-rimmed. She had changed into silk pajamas, her hair pulled back in a loose ponytail that made her look younger than her thirty-seven years.

"Mom? Is everything okay?"

"Can I come in?" Tessa asked, her voice softer than her knocking had been.

Kelly stepped aside, gesturing her mother into the compact but elegantly appointed suite. The balcony door stood ajar, letting in the whisper of the Mediterranean night.

Tessa took a deep breath. "I'm sorry, Kelly. I've let all this drama with Patrick and Richard and everything else get in the way of what matters most: you and me having real time together." She moved to the small sofa, patting the space beside her. "I've been distracted when I should have been listening."

Kelly hesitated before joining her mother. "It's okay. You're on vacation."

"No, it's not okay," Tessa said firmly. "You are the most important person in my life. You always will be. Nothing changes that… not my retirement, not this cruise, not anything." She reached for her daughter's hand. "I know you were trying to tell me something important earlier, and I'm here now. No distractions. No interruptions."

Kelly rose abruptly, pacing the small cabin. She twisted her hands together, a childhood habit Tessa hadn't seen in years.

"I don't know why this is so hard," Kelly muttered. "I'm not ashamed. I'm not confused. I'm happy."

"Then I'm happy too," Tessa said simply.

Kelly stopped pacing and looked directly at her mother. "Briana isn't just my roommate. She's my partner. We've been together for almost two years."

The words hung in the air between them, not as heavy as Kelly had feared they might be.

"She's beautiful," Tessa said, remembering the glimpse of the photo on Kelly's phone. "And clearly makes you happy."

Kelly's eyes widened slightly, then she continued, words tumbling out faster now. "She's brilliant, Mom. So smart, she runs a wellness center in the Mission District. She's funny and optimistic, and she sees the world differently than I do." A smile spread across Kelly's face, her eyes lighting up. "Actually, she reminds me a lot of Aunt Seren. That same energy, you know? That way of making everything seem possible."

Tessa nodded, recognizing the glow of love in her daughter's expression.

"We want to get married," Kelly blurted out. "Next spring. That's why I came on this cruise; I wanted to tell you in person."

Tessa felt a momentary flash of surprise, not at Kelly's sexuality, which she now realized she had perhaps always known on some level, but at the seriousness of the relationship. Her independent daughter, planning a wedding.

"I would very much like to meet the woman who has captured my daughter's heart," Tessa said warmly. "Your sexual identity doesn't change anything between us, Kelly. It's just one more part of who you are, and I love who you are."

Kelly's shoulders relaxed visibly. "I should have told you sooner. I kept waiting for the right moment."

"Sometimes there is no perfect moment," Tessa replied. "We just have to make the moment perfect ourselves."

Kelly laughed, wiping away a stray tear. "That sounds like something Briana would say."

"Then I like her already."

They moved to the balcony, where the night air wrapped around them like a warm embrace. The moon cast a silver path across the water, guiding them onward.

"Tell me everything," Tessa said, settling into a deck chair. "How you met, your first date, when you knew she was the one."

Kelly poured them both glasses of water from the carafe by her bed and began her story. "We met at a climate tech conference in Palo Alto. She was there promoting sustainable wellness practices…"

The hours slipped by as Kelly shared her love story: their first apartment hunt, Briana's terrible cooking but amazing baking skills, and their complementary work schedules. Tessa listened, asked questions, and gradually built a picture of the life her daughter had created.

As the ship cut through the dark waters toward Portofino, mother and daughter reconnected in a way they hadn't in years, not as lawyer and businesswoman, but simply as two women sharing the universal experience of loving and being loved.

* * *

Tessa awoke with a crick in her neck, momentarily disoriented by the unfamiliar ceiling. She was curled awkwardly on Kelly's cabin sofa, her legs tucked beneath a light throw blanket she didn't remember pulling over herself. The gentle rocking of the ship and the distant hum of engines reminded her where she was.

On the bed, Kelly lay sprawled diagonally across the mattress, one arm flung over her face in a sleeping posture Tessa recognized from her daughter's childhood. The clock on the nightstand showed 7:15 AM; they'd talked until nearly three.

Tessa extracted herself from the sofa carefully, wincing as her stiff muscles protested. She tiptoed to the bathroom, splashing cold water on her face and finger-combing her silver hair into some semblance of order. Her reflection showed smudged mascara and pillow creases on her cheek, but also a lightness she hadn't felt in years.

Behind her, Kelly stirred with a groan. "What ungodly hour is it?" she mumbled, rolling over and stretching like a cat.

"Time for the living to join the day," Tessa said, her voice scratchy from sleep.

"We're supposed to meet Julia and Seren for breakfast in about an hour before our Portofino excursion."

Kelly sat up, her hair a wild tangle around her face. "I need coffee before I face Seren's morning energy."

"You and me both," Tessa laughed, reaching for the room service menu. "I should probably head back to my cabin to change."

Kelly studied her mother in the soft morning light filtering through the balcony door. "You know, we never really finished talking about you and the captain."

Tessa busied herself with the coffee maker on the small desk. "There's nothing much to say. I enjoy his company very much, but until I know just how involved he is in this men-for-hire scheme, I can't get too close."

"And now that Gloria and Richard's situation has been explained?" Kelly prompted.

"I'm glad they're safe and Gloria is recovering, but," Tessa said, measuring coffee grounds with careful precision, "that doesn't mean Manny isn't facilitating these connections."

Kelly pulled her knees to her chest, looking suddenly vulnerable despite her executive confidence. "You're entitled to find love, too, Mom. I hope you know that."

Tessa's hands stilled over the coffee maker. Love. Such a simple word for such a complicated feeling.

"I'm not sure that's what this is," she said carefully.

"Maybe not," Kelly shrugged. "But whatever it is… attraction, companionship, just having fun, you deserve it." She leaned forward. "I spent years watching you put yourself second. First for your career, then for me."

"I never regretted any of that," Tessa said firmly.

"I know. That's why you deserve this time for yourself now." Kelly's smile turned mischievous. "Besides, the captain is hot. In a distinguished, silver-fox way."

"Kelly!" Tessa felt heat rise to her cheeks even as she laughed.

Across the ship, Julia and Seren were already awake, sharing coffee on Julia's balcony as Portofino's colorful harbor came into view. Below them on the promenade deck, Captain Delgado conducted his morning inspection, pausing occasionally to gaze out at the approaching coastline.

In the ship's security office, the chief security officer was reviewing the report on Gloria's medical emergency, making notes about their temporary detention in Porto Cervo. And in the crew bar, Miguel was telling Liam about the excitement of the previous evening, their fingers intertwined beneath the table.

The Aurelia glided smoothly through the water, carrying all these stories, some just beginning, some long in progress, toward the picturesque harbor ahead. The Italian coastline shimmered in the morning sun like a promise of beauty yet to come.

Tessa handed Kelly a steaming mug of coffee. "So, what do you think about a spring wedding? I assume Seren will insist on helping plan it."

Kelly grimaced. "God help us all if she does. Briana and I were thinking something small."

"Good luck with that once Seren hears the news," Tessa laughed, settling beside her daughter on the bed. "You might as well resign yourself now to crystal healing stations and organic, fair-trade confetti."

"Hey, Mom," Kelly sounded solemn. "Do you mind if I tell Aunt Seren and Aunt Julia?"

"Absolutely not." Tessa grinned, "But you better hurry. I don't know how long I can keep a secret. They're going to wonder why I'm smiling this morning."

As they shared quiet laughter and coffee in the morning light, Tessa felt a sensation of rightness settle over her. Whatever uncertainties lay ahead, with the captain, with retirement, with this next chapter of her life, she knew with absolute certainty that this bond with her daughter would remain her truest north star.

Chapter 11

The tender bobbed gently against the waves as it ferried passengers from the Aurelia toward Portofino's picture-perfect harbor. Tessa sat between Kelly and Julia; her face tilted toward the warming sun. Around them, the sparkling azure water reflected a kaleidoscope of pastel-colored buildings that seemed to climb the hillside like a painter's dream.

"I've never seen anything so beautiful," Julia breathed, her writer's eye cataloging every detail.

Liam slipped into an empty seat across from them, his hair tousled by the sea breeze. "Room for one more wanderer?" He flashed an apologetic smile.

"Of course, we have room for you," Tessa said, surprising herself with her genuine warmth. After last night's revelations and this morning's coffee with Kelly, she felt a new openness toward Liam. "You're practically family now."

Liam's eyes widened slightly before his face broke into a grateful smile. Kelly caught his glance and gave him a tiny nod that didn't escape Tessa's notice.

The tender bumped against the dock, and the small group disembarked into the bustling Piazza Martiri dell'Olivetta. The harbor square pulsed with life: tourists sipping espresso at outdoor cafés, locals arranging fresh flowers in window boxes, and fishermen untangling nets while arguing good-naturedly in rapid-fire Italian.

"The colors are unbelievable," Seren exclaimed, her bohemian dress swirling around her ankles as she spun to take it all in. "This is what living looks like!"

They wandered through narrow cobblestone streets, pausing to admire handcrafted jewelry and artisanal olive oils displayed in tiny shop windows. Julia snapped photos at every turn while Seren engaged shopkeepers in animated conversation despite language barriers.

As they began the gentle climb up the path toward the Church of San Giorgio, Kelly fell into step beside her mother. "Did you talk to the captain this morning?" she asked quietly.

Tessa shook her head. "He was busy with the docking procedures. I'll find him later."

"Make sure you do," Kelly replied with a meaningful look. "No more letting other people's drama distract you from what matters."

Ahead of them, the simple whitewashed façade of the church came into view, standing sentinel over the harbor. They climbed the last few steps and paused to catch their breath, turning to admire the spectacular vista spreading below them, the harbor's horseshoe shape now fully visible, dotted with boats that looked like toys from this height.

Inside the church, cool shadows and silence enveloped them. The modest interior was a stark contrast to Italy's more ornate cathedrals, but its simplicity held its own kind of grace. Seren drifted toward a bank of votive candles while Julia examined the artwork on the walls.

Kelly tugged gently at Seren's flowing sleeve. "Aunt Seren, Aunt Julia, can I talk to you for a minute?"

Tessa caught her daughter's eye and nodded encouragingly before walking with Liam toward the church entrance, giving them privacy.

In the quiet corner near the altar, Kelly took a deep breath. "I have some news," she began, her voice steady despite the slight tremor in her hands. "I wanted to tell you both that I'm engaged."

Julia's eyebrows rose in surprise. "Engaged? But I thought…"

"Her name is Briana," Kelly continued, her face softening at the name. "We've been together for almost two years, and we're planning to get married next spring."

A beat of silence passed before Seren broke into a radiant smile. "Oh, my darling girl!" She enveloped Kelly in a fierce hug, her collection of bracelets jangling. "That's absolutely wonderful news!"

Julia joined the embrace, her eyes shining. "I couldn't be happier for you, Kelly."

"So you're not… surprised?" Kelly asked, extricating herself from their arms.

"That you're marrying a woman?" Julia tilted her head thoughtfully. "Perhaps a little. That you've found someone who makes you happy? Not at all."

"Love is love, sweetheart," Seren added, clasping Kelly's hands. "And the universe has clearly guided you to your person."

Kelly laughed, relief evident in her relaxed shoulders. "Mom said the same thing… well, minus the universe part."

"Speaking of weddings," Seren's eyes lit up with excitement, "I know the most amazing venue in Sedona. The energy vortexes there would create such a powerful foundation for your union. And for the ceremony itself, I'm thinking crystal meditation stations, a blessing circle with sacred sage…"

"Whoa, slow down," Kelly interrupted with an amused smile. "Briana and I were thinking something small. And we need to include her in these decisions."

"Of course, of course," Seren waved dismissively. "But small doesn't mean it can't be spiritually significant. I'll start a Pinterest board immediately."

Julia gently steered them back toward the entrance, where Tessa and Liam waited. "Let's continue this wedding planning as we walk. I think we're holding up the tour."

Outside in the sunshine, Liam managed to catch Kelly alone for a moment as they climbed toward Castle Brown. "So? How did it go?" he asked quietly.

Kelly's smile was an answer enough. "You were right. Everyone's been amazing."

"Told you," he replied with a gentle nudge to her shoulder. "Coming out to supportive people is like finally exhaling after holding your breath underwater. Trust me, I know."

"Thank you," Kelly said simply. "For being a friend when I needed one this week."

The group continued their exploration, wandering through Castle Brown's lush gardens and taking dozens of photos of the panoramic views. As the afternoon sun reached its zenith, they made their way back down to the harbor, where Tessa insisted on treating everyone to lunch at Ristorante Puny.

"This calls for champagne," she announced as they settled at a prime table overlooking the water. When the waiter appeared, she ordered their finest bottle. "We're celebrating my daughter's engagement."

As the cork popped and bubbles fizzed into crystal flutes, Tessa raised her glass. The sunlight caught in the champagne, creating tiny rainbows that danced across the white tablecloth.

"To Kelly and Briana," she toasted, her voice carrying the weight of maternal pride. "May your life together be as beautiful as this day."

"To Kelly and Briana!" the others echoed, clinking glasses.

Around them, Portofino continued its timeless dance: fishermen mending nets, children licking gelato cones, lovers stealing kisses in shadowed doorways. The Aurelia waited patiently in the harbor, ready to carry them to their next destination. But for this golden afternoon, time seemed suspended in the Italian sunshine as they celebrated love in all its unexpected forms.

Under the table, Tessa's phone buzzed with a message from Captain Delgado, "Dinner tonight? Just the two of us this time."

She smiled and slipped the phone back into her purse. There would be time for that later. Right now, this moment with her daughter, her dearest friends, and their newfound companion was exactly where she needed to be.

* * *

The Mediterranean sun began its gentle descent as the group meandered along the lighthouse path, dappled shadows playing across their faces. Pine and olive trees lined the trail, offering welcome respite from the afternoon heat while framing spectacular views of the sparkling sea below. Laughter floated between them, lighter and more carefree than it had been all week.

"I still can't believe Seren offered to officiate wearing 'ceremonial robes of transformation,'" Julia said, her eyes crinkling with amusement.

"I'm more concerned about the crystal grid she wants to install under the dance floor," Kelly replied, shaking her head. "Briana might actually go for that part, though."

Tessa watched her daughter's face glow as she spoke about her fiancée, a warmth spreading through her chest that had nothing to do with the Italian sunshine. She'd never seen Kelly quite this unguarded, this willing to share her joy.

They reached the lighthouse café, a charming stone building with a terrace overlooking the endless blue expanse. Small tables dotted with bright yellow umbrellas beckoned them forward.

"Limoncello?" Seren suggested, already guiding them toward a table with the best view. "It feels positively criminal to be in Italy and not partake."

Just as they settled into their seats, Kelly's phone buzzed. Her face lit up as she checked the screen. "It's Briana," she said, standing quickly. "Do you mind if I…"

"Go," Tessa urged with a smile. "Tell her we're drinking to her health."

Kelly stepped away, phone pressed to her ear, her voice carrying fragments of excited conversation back to them. Within minutes, she returned, her smile even wider.

"She wants to say hello to everyone," Kelly announced, switching her phone to camera mode. "Wave and say hi!"

The group clustered together, faces bright as Kelly panned across them with her camera. "Hello, Briana!" they called in cheerful unison.

"Congratulations!" Seren added with particular enthusiasm. "I've already started planning your crystal ceremony!"

Kelly rolled her eyes but couldn't suppress her smile as she returned to her conversation, stepping away again to finish the call in private.

"She looks so happy," Tessa said softly, watching her daughter's animated gestures as she spoke into the phone. "I can't remember the last time I saw her like this."

Julia reached across the table and squeezed Tessa's hand. "You raised an amazing woman, Tess. Strong enough to forge her own path, brave enough to be herself."

"And smart enough to find someone who appreciates her," Seren added, raising her small glass of limoncello. "To finding true partners at any age."

They clinked glasses, the sweet citrus liqueur warming their throats as they savored both the moment and the view. Kelly rejoined them, slipping her phone back into her pocket with a contented sigh.

The late afternoon stretched lazily before them as they made their way back down to the harbor, no one in any particular hurry to end their perfect day. The water taxi awaited to take them back to the Aurelia, bobbing gently against the dock.

As they stepped aboard, Tessa froze momentarily, recognizing a familiar profile among the seated passengers. Richard Collier sat alone near the stern; his attention fixed on the water. The group exchanged glances before finding seats nearby.

"Richard," Tessa ventured after a moment, "how is Gloria doing? We were all quite concerned."

He turned, surprise registering briefly on his face before settling into a practiced smile. "She's stable and expected to make a full recovery. Her family is flying in today to be with her."

"What happened exactly?" Julia asked, her writer's curiosity evident.

"Severe food reaction," Richard replied smoothly. "The local doctor said it might have been cross-contamination with shellfish. She's terribly allergic."

Kelly's eyes narrowed slightly, but she said nothing. The tender lurched gently as it pulled away from the dock, Portofino's colorful façades receding into a picture-postcard view.

"Will you be continuing the cruise?" Seren inquired, bracelets jingling as she adjusted her flowing scarf.

"Of course," Richard nodded. "Gloria insisted. No sense in both of us missing the rest of this beautiful journey."

The conversation lapsed into polite silence as the tender made its way across the harbor toward the waiting Aurelia. Tessa couldn't help noticing how Richard's gaze kept returning to the ship with an expression she couldn't quite read—anticipation, perhaps, or calculation.

Back onboard, they dispersed to their respective cabins to freshen up before dinner. In the elevator, Liam leaned close to Kelly and whispered something that made her laugh. Julia and Seren debated whether to try the French restaurant or return to the Italian venue they'd enjoyed earlier in the cruise.

Tessa's thoughts, however, had already drifted to her upcoming dinner with Manny.

* * *

The Celestial Lounge glowed with subdued elegance as night fell over the Mediterranean. Floor-to-ceiling windows revealed the darkening waters outside, mirroring the twinkling lights arranged tastefully throughout the space. A pianist played gentle jazz classics, providing the perfect backdrop for intimate conversation

Tessa, Julia, Seren, and Kelly had secured a corner banquette with plush velvet seating and a low marble table now adorned with their assorted cocktails. Kelly's fingers occasionally strayed to her phone, no doubt checking for messages from Briana.

"I still can't believe Richard just appeared on that tender," Seren remarked, stirring her martini with practiced flair. "Something doesn't add up about his story."

"Allergic reaction," Julia mused. "Convenient explanation that's hard to disprove."

Tessa opened her mouth to respond when she noticed Liam approaching their table with purpose in his stride. He slipped into the empty space beside Kelly, his expression a mixture of excitement and caution.

"Ladies," he said, leaning forward conspiratorially and lowering his voice. "I've just spoken with Miguel. Two Interpol agents boarded the ship in Portofino this afternoon."

The group fell silent, exchanging startled glances.

"Interpol?" Kelly whispered. "Are they here for Patrick?"

Liam shook his head. "Apparently, some very valuable jewelry has gone missing from a couple of staterooms. High-end stuff: diamonds, emeralds. One passenger reported losing pieces worth over two hundred thousand euros."

Tessa's shoulders slumped slightly. "I was hoping they were finally onto Patrick and his scam."

"Theft on a luxury cruise," Julia muttered, taking a thoughtful sip of her wine.

"This could be devastating for Selene Voyages if word gets out. First, these lotharios preying on wealthy women, now valuable jewelry disappearing from supposedly secure staterooms."

"Reputation is everything in luxury travel," Seren agreed. "One scandal can sink years of carefully cultivated prestige."

Tessa traced the rim of her glass with her fingertip. "Poor Manny. This isn't even his regular ship. He's just filling in while the Iridessa is in dry dock, and now he's dealing with lotharios, missing passengers, and Interpol investigations."

Kelly's eyebrows shot up. "Well, well. You've gone from suspecting the captain of running a gigolo ring to worrying about his professional reputation. That's quite the turnaround, Mom."

A flush crept up Tessa's neck. "I'm simply acknowledging the difficult position he's in. It doesn't mean I've completely dismissed my concerns."

"But you're having dinner with him tonight," Kelly pressed, a knowing smile playing at her lips.

"Speaking of which," Liam interrupted, placing his hand on Tessa's arm, "please don't mention any of this to the captain. Miguel wasn't supposed to tell me about the Interpol agents. The officers are traveling undercover, and only senior staff know they're aboard. If Manny finds out Miguel's been talking, he could lose his position."

"Of course I won't say anything," Tessa assured him. "But if there's a jewel thief on board targeting wealthy passengers, shouldn't people be warned?"

Julia glanced around the lounge, her writer's eye assessing the other passengers with new suspicion. "A thief, a lothario, and now Interpol. This cruise has turned into quite the mystery novel."

"And we're right in the middle of it," Seren said, raising her glass. "To unexpected adventures."

They clinked glasses, the tension momentarily broken by Seren's toast. But as Tessa checked her watch and realized it was nearly time to meet Manny, she couldn't help wondering what other secrets the Aurelia might be harboring beneath its polished surface.

Chapter 12

The Terrazza di Mare restaurant glowed with warm amber lighting that complemented the rich wood paneling and polished brass fixtures. Outside the windows, the endless expanse of the Mediterranean had transformed into a canvas of indigo dotted with the distant lights of coastal towns. The dining room buzzed with the gentle hum of conversation and the occasional clink of fine crystal.

At a secluded corner table, Tessa and Manny sat across from each other, the remnants of their seafood linguine pushed aside. Between them, a candle flickered in a small glass hurricane, casting a golden glow across their faces. Manny had loosened his tie slightly, and the tension that had marked his posture throughout dinner had eased somewhat.

"You haven't mentioned the missing passengers," Tessa remarked, taking a sip of her Barolo. "I heard Richard Collier returned today, but Gloria is still hospitalized?"

Manny nodded, his silver hair catching the candlelight. "Sí, Richard returned alone. Gloria suffered a severe allergic reaction, nothing sinister, thankfully. Her family arrived to be with her at the hospital." He swirled the wine in his glass thoughtfully. "These things happen on cruises, unfortunately. People forget medications, eat something they shouldn't…"

The sommelier approached their table with practiced discretion, presenting a dessert menu that Manny waved away with a polite smile.

"We've already decided," he said. "The chocolate soufflé for the lady, and I'll have the panna cotta with fresh berries."

When the sommelier departed, Tessa leaned slightly forward. "It was kind of you to delay the ship's departure for them. I understand that's not standard procedure."

"Sometimes exceptions must be made," Manny replied with a small shrug. "Especially for valued guests."

Across the restaurant, the maître d' greeted a couple entering for a late dinner. At another table, a woman laughed too loudly at her companion's joke. A server dropped a fork with a soft clatter, quickly replacing it. The background noises created a cocoon of privacy around their conversation.

"I've been thinking about what you told me earlier," Tessa said, her fingers tracing the stem of her wine glass. "About your childhood in Positano. I'd like to see it someday; experience it through your eyes."

Something in Manny's expression softened. "I would like that very much. The views from my family's olive grove… they cannot be captured in photographs." His hand moved across the table, his fingers lightly brushing against hers. "Perhaps one day…"

A crisp-uniformed junior officer approached their table with the stiff posture of someone carrying unwelcome news. He hesitated briefly, noticing the intimate moment he was interrupting.

"Excuse me, Captain. I apologize for the intrusion."

Manny's expression flickered with irritation before settling into professional composure. He straightened in his chair, the captain's persona sliding back into place like a well-worn uniform.

"Yes, Ensign Torres?"

"Sir, you're needed in your office immediately. It's… urgent." The young officer's eyes darted briefly toward Tessa, then back to the captain, clearly communicating that this was not a matter for public discussion.

Throughout the dining room, several passengers noticed the exchange, their attention drawn to the captain's table with undisguised curiosity. In the world of luxury cruising, any deviation from routine sparked interest and speculation.

Manny nodded crisply. "I'll be there shortly."

The ensign gave a small bow and retreated, leaving Manny and Tessa alone again, though the intimate atmosphere had evaporated. Around them, diners pretended to return to their conversations while stealing glances at their table.

Manny turned back to Tessa, genuine regret etched across his features. "I am so sorry, Cara. This happens sometimes."

"The burden of command," Tessa replied with an understanding smile, though her mind was already racing with possibilities. The missing jewelry, perhaps? Or had the real purpose of the "Interpol agents" been discovered?

Manny signaled to the server. "Please ensure Mrs. Monroe's dessert is served promptly. She is not to wait."

"Of course, Captain."

He turned back to Tessa, taking her hand properly now. "Please, enjoy your soufflé. If I can get away later, perhaps we could meet for a nightcap?"

The warmth of his hand around hers momentarily pushed aside her suspicions. "I'd like that," she heard herself say.

"Bene." He squeezed her hand gently before releasing it. "If I cannot make it, I will send word."

As he stood, he straightened his jacket with a practiced motion, instantly transforming Manny back into Captain Delgado. With a small bow, he departed, nodding politely to other diners as he made his way through the restaurant.

Tessa watched him go, her thoughts churning beneath her composed exterior. What urgent matter could require the captain's immediate attention this late in the evening? Was it related to the jewelry thefts Liam had mentioned? Or perhaps Patrick Desmond had finally made a move obvious enough to warrant intervention?

Her chocolate soufflé arrived, a perfect dome dusted with powdered sugar, served with a small pitcher of warm vanilla crème anglaise. The server poured the sauce with a flourish, creating a small pool around the base of the dessert.

"The captain sends his apologies again, madame. May I bring you an after-dinner liqueur to accompany your dessert? Perhaps a Vin Santo or Grand Marnier?"

"No, thank you," Tessa replied, her appetite for both dessert and alcohol suddenly diminished.

As she dipped her spoon into the soufflé, watching the chocolate center ooze out to mingle with the vanilla sauce, she realized that despite her lingering doubts about Manny's involvement with Patrick and the others, she was disappointed by the interruption. More than that, she was looking forward to seeing him again later, even as part of her brain cautioned against trusting too easily.

She took a bite of the soufflé, barely tasting its rich flavor as she wondered what secrets lurked behind the Aurelia's shiny façade and how many of them Manny was keeping from her.

* * *

Manny walked swiftly through the corridors of the Aurelia, nodding curtly to passing crew members who quickly stepped aside. His mind remained split between the dinner he'd just left and the meeting ahead. The weight of command settled heavily on his shoulders, a familiar burden, but one made heavier by personal complications.

He'd been looking forward to that soufflé with Tessa. More than that, he'd been looking forward to what might have followed, perhaps a walk along the moonlit deck, her hand in his, the Mediterranean breeze carrying the promise of something more. There had been a moment, just before Torres arrived, when Tessa had looked at him with such openness that Manny had allowed himself to imagine possibilities beyond this voyage.

Life had a particular talent for timing, he reflected wryly.

When Interpol had approached him just a week ago about temporarily taking command of the Aurelia after Grimaldi had been relieved and to help catch this ring of predators Grimaldi was apparently involved with, he'd agreed without hesitation. It was the right thing to do. Then fate had placed Tessa Monroe on his passenger manifest, and suddenly duty had become considerably more complicated.

He reached his office door and paused, taking a deep breath to center himself. Inside waited representatives from two international law enforcement agencies and a case that spanned three continents. He needed his full attention on the task at hand, not on a pair of intelligent eyes and the way they crinkled slightly at the corners when she smiled.

"Captain," Agent Diane Harris of the FBI greeted him as he entered. Her tailored pantsuit couldn't quite disguise her athletic build, and her expression was all business. Beside her stood Interpol Agent Marceau, his posture rigid even while seated.

"We have confirmation," Marceau said without preamble. "Gloria Sullivan was drugged. The hospital toxicology report shows benzodiazepines in her system, not food poisoning as Collier claimed."

Manny's jaw tightened. "She will recover?"

"Yes. Fortunately, she realized something was wrong and got herself to a clinic before losing consciousness completely." Harris pulled out her tablet. "We believe Collier got her to compromise her accounts while she was incapacitated; she would not have noticed anything unusual until she returned home if we had not been tracking Richard."

"Our colleagues in Italy are monitoring her financial accounts," Marceau added.

"And what of Captain Grimaldi?" Manny asked, settling into his chair.

Harris slid a folder across the desk. "Substantial evidence. Not only was he receiving kickbacks from Desmond, Collier and others for identifying potential targets, but we've linked him to jewelry thefts on four separate voyages. Captain Grimaldi took a percentage of whatever they sold the jewels for."

"And the crew member working with them?"

"Housekeeping Manager Putu Amurao." Harris displayed a surveillance photo on her tablet. "He's been with Selene Voyages for three years. We believe he's responsible for at least twelve cabin breaches."

Manny nodded grimly. Another betrayal of trust, another officer using his position to prey on those who relied on him. The thought made his stomach turn.

"And Ms. Rothschild? How is she holding up?"

Something like respect flickered across Harris's face. "Vivian's a pro. Twenty-seven years with the Bureau before retirement. When we approached her about this operation, she didn't hesitate."

"She's played a good role," Marceau added. "Building his trust, playing the wealthy widow. When we port in Marseille, she'll wire him two hundred fifty thousand dollars for his supposed investment opportunity."

"Why can't it be done in Nice?" Manny posed a logical question.

"It takes a day or two for the FBI to move the funds into a dummy account," Harris explained. "We'll use that account to wire the money to Desmond."

"And that's when you move in?" Manny asked.

Harris nodded. "We have enough on Collier and Kuester now to arrest him, but Desmond is the bigger fish. He's been doing this for years, changing identities, targeting women across three continents. The money Vivian wires will give us the final evidence we need."

"We appreciate your discretion, Captain," Marceau said. "We know this operation has disrupted your ship's routine."

Manny thought of Tessa, of her suspicions about his involvement with these men, how he'd had to deflect her concerns without revealing the truth. "It's been… challenging," he admitted.

"Just two more days," Harris assured him. "Once we make the arrests in Marseille, you can get back to normal."

* * *

Manny took a steadying breath and dialed Tessa's number on the house phone, the low hum of the ship thrumming beneath his feet. When she answered, he could almost feel her warmth through the line.

"Tessa, it's Manny. Need some fresh air," he began, trying to mask the fatigue heavy in his voice. "Would you join me for a nightcap on deck? I promise not to keep you long."

"Of course, Manny," came her reply, gentle and understanding. "I could use the fresh air too."

Minutes later, they met on the vacant crew deck beneath the bridge. Manny had brought along a bottle of bourbon and a couple of glasses. The sea stretched vast and inky black around them, the sky peppered with stars that flickered like tiny beacons against the void.

Tessa settled against the railing, cradling her glass, allowing the silence to wrap around them. Her gaze, steady and knowing, fell on Manny, granting him the space he needed to find his words.

"Forgive me for leaving you at dinner," he eventually said, the regret evident. "I promise, we'll have a proper meal soon. Without interruption."

Her smile was soft, reassuring. "I understand," she murmured. "The responsibilities you hold… they're not just duties, they're burdens."

Manny nodded, the bourbon burning a comforting path down his throat. "There are matters, pressing ones, that demand my attention. I wish I had more time," he paused, watching as the waves shimmered in the moonlight, "to spend with you."

Tessa remained silent, allowing him to continue at his own pace. The wind tousled her hair, but she made no move to tame it, her focus on Manny and the tension etched into the corners of his eyes.

"I'm not at liberty to discuss the details," he said, turning to face her, his gaze earnest. "But I assure you, matters will resolve in the coming days."

She nodded, her expression one of deep understanding. "I've carried my own set of burdens as managing partner at a law firm," she shared, the weight of her past roles reflected in her voice. "There were always secrets."

A playful glint sparked in her eyes. "But you know," she teased, gesturing to her glass, "if you toss me a dollar as a retainer, I might just be bound to attorney-client confidentiality."

Manny chuckled, feeling some of the day's weight lift, at least for this moment. Her presence, steadfast and calming, offered a refuge, a reminder of connection amidst chaos.

Chapter 13

The morning broke over Nice with a gentle kiss of light, bathing the Promenade des Anglais in a warm, golden glow. The group of five, which now included Liam by default, strolled along the famous walkway, the Mediterranean stretching before them in a tapestry of blues, from turquoise near the shore to deep sapphire at the horizon. Seagulls swooped and called overhead, their cries mingling with the soft murmur of waves against the pebbled beach.

"Now this," Seren declared, spreading her arms wide as if to embrace the entire coastline, "is exactly what retirement should look like." Her bohemian dress fluttered in the sea breeze, catching the light like stained glass.

Julia snapped photos of everything, the ornate Belle Époque buildings, the palm trees standing sentinel along the promenade, and especially her friends. Her fingers occasionally paused to jot notes in her small leather-bound notebook. "I'm seeing at least three potential story settings already," she murmured, her artistic mind transforming the scenery into narrative landscapes.

They found a charming café with tables spilling onto the sidewalk. The scent of freshly baked pastries and rich coffee enveloped them as they settled into their chairs.

"I could get used to this," Kelly sighed, breaking off a piece of her pain au chocolat. The morning sun caught in her blonde waves, highlighting the contentment on her face, a marked change from the woman who'd been constantly checking her phone just days earlier.

"Speaking of things to get used to," Tessa began, stirring her café crème, "have you and Briana set a date yet?"

Kelly's smile widened. "We're thinking spring. Nothing too elaborate, maybe fifty people at most."

"Fifty?" Seren looked scandalized. "That's practically eloping! At least let me help with a proper venue. I know people."

Liam chuckled, his eyes crinkling at the corners. "Careful what you agree to, Kelly, I have a feeling Seren's idea of 'not elaborate' might involve imported flowers and doves released at sunset."

They finished their breakfast and wandered into the labyrinthine streets of Vieux Nice, where buildings in shades of ochre, terracotta, and amber pressed close together, creating a patchwork of warm color against the bright blue sky. The narrow alleyways offered shade and discovery; tiny shops selling everything from handmade soaps to intricate jewelry.

The Cours Saleya market buzzed with life. Vendors called out their wares in melodic French, the air thick with the perfume of fresh flowers, herbs, and ripe fruits. Julia bought a small bunch of lavender, tucking a sprig behind her ear.

"So, Kelly," she asked, pausing before a display of vibrant flowers, "traditional white wedding, or something more adventurous?"

Kelly fingered a stem of deep purple anemones. "Briana wants something colorful. She says white is overrated."

"Smart woman," Seren nodded approvingly. "I like her already."

Tessa watched her daughter with quiet joy, seeing how freely Kelly now spoke of her future. The tension that had clouded their relationship had lifted, replaced by an easy openness that felt like a gift.

Liam stopped before a stall selling olive oils and vinegars. "Try this," he insisted, offering them each a piece of bread dipped in a golden-green oil. "The vendor says it's from a small family farm just outside the city."

* * *

The olive oil bloomed across Kelly's tongue, a complex symphony of peppery and fruity notes that lingered pleasantly. "This is incredible," she murmured, accepting another piece of bread from the vendor.

"Wait, isn't that Richard Collier?" Kelly suddenly straightened, her attention drawn across the bustling market square.

The group followed her gaze to see Richard emerging from a bank, tucking his wallet into his inside jacket pocket. His movements were quick, almost furtive, as he glanced around before heading in the opposite direction.

"Wonder what he's doing here alone," Tessa mused, thanking the vendor as they stepped away from the olive oil display.

Julia's observant eyes narrowed. "He's not alone, or at least, not unaccompanied." She nodded discreetly toward a man in a linen shirt and sunglasses, about thirty feet behind Richard. "That man has been matching Richard's pace since he left the exchange."

"Are you sure?" Seren squinted in the bright Mediterranean light.

"Positive. He's maintaining the same distance, slowing when Richard slows, speeding up when he does." Julia's writer's instincts for detail kicked in. "And he's been adjusting his sunglasses unnecessarily; it's a nervous tick when someone's focused on surveillance."

"I've seen him before," Liam said quietly, his voice dropping to barely above a whisper. "On the ship. He keeps to himself, but I've noticed him at the bar a few times, always watching the room."

The five of them stood frozen in momentary indecision until Tessa broke the spell with a mischievous smile. "Well, this day just got considerably more interesting."

As if by unspoken agreement, they began drifting in the same direction Richard and his shadow had taken, maintaining a careful distance.

"Are we actually following them?" Kelly asked, fighting a grin.

"Call it... professional curiosity," Tessa replied, her eyes never leaving Richard's retreating figure.

They wove through the colorful streets of Nice's Old Town, past shops selling lavender soaps and boutiques displaying handcrafted jewelry. Occasionally, they paused at a storefront, pretending to admire merchandise while keeping track of their quarry.

"He's heading toward Place Garibaldi," Liam observed as they turned onto a wider boulevard. "Lots of restaurants there."

Sure enough, Richard eventually settled at an outdoor table at Chez Acchiardo, a charming traditional restaurant tucked into a quiet corner of the square. The historic eatery, with its cheerful red awning and stone facade weathered by centuries of Mediterranean sun, looked like it had been serving locals since before tourism existed.

"Now what?" Seren whispered, hiding behind an enormous pair of sunglasses.

"Now we have lunch," Tessa decided, steering them toward a table with a clear sightline to Richard but far enough away to avoid detection. "And observe."

The mysterious follower had positioned himself at a nearby café, looking intently at his phone while keeping Richard in his peripheral vision. Several minutes later, an athletically built woman, stylishly dressed, slid into a seat at his table.

"This is better than any novel I could write," Julia murmured as they settled in and accepted menus.

The restaurant's interior spilled out into the square, with checkered tablecloths and wicker chairs creating an atmosphere of casual Niçoise elegance. Overhead, strings of lights waited for the evening to transform the space into something magical. The scent of garlic, fresh herbs, and olive oil perfumed the air.

"Bonjour! Bienvenue à Chez Acchiardo," their waiter greeted them warmly. "C'est une belle journée, non?"

They ordered a feast of local specialties: salade niçoise with fresh-caught tuna, pan bagnat sandwiches bursting with olives and anchovies, socca (the region's famous chickpea pancakes), and a carafe of chilled rosé that glowed pink in the sunlight.

"That man is definitely tracking Richard," Kelly observed between bites of her crisp, herb-infused socca. "He hasn't touched his espresso, and looks up every couple of minutes."

"I'm guessing Interpol agents," Liam said quietly, leaning in so only their table could hear. "They must be a team."

"You seem to know a lot about international police operations," Seren remarked, eyebrows raised.

Liam shrugged, a half-smile playing on his lips. "I read a lot of thrillers."

"Whatever's happening, I think we should keep our distance," Tessa decided, watching as Richard paid his bill and prepared to leave. "If this is an official investigation, the last thing we want is to interfere."

"Agreed," Julia nodded. "Though I'm taking mental notes for my next book."

"Look," Kelly whispered. The woman with the shadow man tucked her phone into her purse and stood. She followed at a careful distance as Richard began strolling toward the harbor. The man waited several minutes before following behind them.

"Should we follow?" Seren asked, excitement dancing in her eyes.

"No," Tessa said firmly, refilling their wine glasses. "Liam's right. If this is Interpol, we need to stay out of it. Besides," she added with a smile, "I'm not done enjoying this remarkable lunch in this beautiful place with all of you."

As their conversation drifted to other topics—Kelly's wedding plans, Julia's writing projects, and Seren's retreat ideas—Tessa couldn't help occasionally glancing in the direction Richard had disappeared. The mystery of it all lingered in her mind, another piece in the increasingly complex puzzle of their Mediterranean cruise.

The warm Niçoise sun bathed them in golden light as they finished their meal, momentarily forgetting about lotharios and undercover agents and jewelry thefts. For now, they were simply friends enjoying a perfect day in France, their glasses filled with rosé the color of sunset and their hearts lightened by shared adventure.

* * *

After lunch, they wandered through Nice's sun-dappled streets with the pleasant weight of good food and wine in their bellies. The afternoon stretched before them like a gift; no responsibilities, no agenda beyond exploration. The heightened excitement of their impromptu surveillance operation had given way to a more languid pleasure in simply being present.

"I think we should visit the Matisse Museum," Julia suggested, consulting a small guidebook she'd tucked in her purse. "It's in the Cimiez neighborhood, up on the hill."

"I vote we take that little tourist train first," Seren pointed to the white-canopied tram that ferried visitors through the city's highlights. "My feet could use a break from all this intrigue."

The Petit Train wound its way through Nice's most picturesque corners, the guide's commentary floating back to them in both French and English. Tessa found herself watching her companions more than the scenery; Kelly's face relaxed and open in a way it hadn't been for years, Julia documenting everything with her writer's eye, Seren's bohemian spirit soaking up each colorful vista, and Liam pointing out architectural details with unexpected knowledge.

They recognized several couples from the ship among the tourists browsing the boutiques and cafés, nodding in acknowledgment but keeping to themselves. Of Richard and his mysterious shadows, there was no sign.

At Castle Hill, they disembarked to explore the ruins and gardens. The climb rewarded them with a panoramic view that stole their breath; the entire curve of the Baie des Anges spread below them like a painting, the Mediterranean stretching to infinity in varying shades of blue.

"It's like looking at a living postcard," Kelly murmured, the breeze lifting her hair. "I need to bring Briana here someday."

Julia captured the scene with her camera while Seren closed her eyes, face tilted toward the sun in quiet meditation. Below them, the terracotta roofs of Old Nice created a patchwork of warmth against the azure backdrop of sea and sky.

"I can see why artists have been drawn to this light for centuries," Julia said, lowering her camera. "There's something about it that transforms the ordinary into something magical."

The afternoon light had indeed taken on that quality peculiar to the Côte d'Azur: a golden luminosity that seemed to intensify colors and soften edges. As they descended from Castle Hill, they found themselves drawn to the artisan shops tucked into the narrow streets of Old Town.

In a tiny ceramic boutique no larger than a ship's cabin, Tessa ran her fingers over hand-painted plates decorated with vibrant olives and lemons. "Mom would have loved these," she murmured, selecting a small olive dish with a delicate pattern of lavender sprigs.

Julia was drawn to a set of ceramic vases in varying shades of Mediterranean blue. "For my writing desk," she explained, as the shopkeeper wrapped them carefully in tissue paper.

Seren discovered a collection of whimsical figurines: mermaids and sea creatures glazed in colors that seemed to capture the essence of the ocean itself. "Perfect for my meditation space," she declared, selecting a serene-faced mermaid with flowing hair.

"This is for Briana," Kelly said softly, holding up a pair of espresso cups painted with wildflowers. "Our first joint possession for our new home together."

They continued their treasure hunt through the winding streets, stopping at a perfumery where the shopkeeper invited them to sample fragrances crafted from locally grown flowers.

"This is pure Nice in a bottle," the woman explained in accented English, dabbing lavender and citrus essence on their wrists. The scent bloomed in the warm air, evoking sunlit fields and sea breezes.

Seren closed her eyes, inhaling deeply. "I'll take two bottles. One for me, one for… future opportunities," she added with a wink that made the others laugh.

By the time they reached the Promenade des Anglais again, the afternoon had mellowed toward evening. Their arms were laden with carefully wrapped packages: ceramics, fragrances, and small treasures that would forever connect them to this day.

"We should head back to the ship," Tessa said reluctantly, watching the light change over the water. "But I feel like we've lived an entire lifetime in just one afternoon."

"That's the magic of travel," Liam offered, helping Julia with her packages. "It expands time somehow."

As they made their way back toward the port, the mystery of Richard Collier and his watchers felt distant and unimportant. What remained was the warmth of friendship, the beauty of their surroundings, and the sweet satisfaction of a day well spent.

The sun hung low over the harbor as they approached the tender station, painting the water and sky in deepening shades of orange and pink. Another perfect Mediterranean day was drawing to a close, adding itself to their collection of shared memories; a treasure far more valuable than any they could carry home in tissue-wrapped boxes.

Chapter 14

Tessa, Julia, Seren, Kelly, and Liam boarded the ship, their shopping bags filled with treasures and their minds with memories. The day's curious observations about Richard Collier had receded somewhat during their afternoon of exploration, but hadn't vanished completely.

"I think I'll head back to my cabin and call Briana before dinner," Kelly said, adjusting her packages as they cleared security. "She'll want to hear about everything we saw today."

"And I need to organize these photos before I forget what's what," Julia added, patting her camera bag. "Meet for pre-dinner drinks at seven?"

As they dispersed toward their respective cabins, the ship hummed with the familiar rhythm of passengers returning, crew members preparing for evening service, and the subtle vibrations of engines maintaining position in the harbor.

Three decks above, in the secure conference room adjacent to the bridge, Captain Manny Delgado settled into his chair at the head of the table. His face revealed nothing as he glanced at the small assembly before him: Agent Marceau from Interpol, FBI Agent Diane Harris, and Chief Security Officer Nikolai Petrov.

"Report," he said simply, his accent thickening slightly with fatigue.

Agent Marceau leaned forward, his lean fingers spreading a series of surveillance photos across the polished table surface. "We successfully tailed Collier to Crédit Agricole in Nice this morning. He transferred forty-seven thousand euros from Gloria Sullivan's account to an account registered to Thomas Evans." His lips thinned with satisfaction. "One of his known aliases, which we've documented in three previous cases."

"The account has been frozen?" Manny asked.

"Within seventeen minutes of the transfer," Marceau confirmed. "Gloria's funds will be fully recovered once we make the arrests. She'll face no financial consequences from this encounter."

Manny nodded, his silver hair catching the light. "And the other matters?"

Diane Harris took over, her voice crisp with professional efficiency. "The dummy account is funded and operational. Tomorrow in Marseille, Vivian will transfer two hundred fifty thousand dollars to Desmond for his supposed AI investment opportunity. Once the transfer clears, we'll have concrete evidence of wire fraud to add to the existing charges."

"She's been remarkably steady throughout this operation," Petrov added, admiration evident in his voice. "Most civilians would have cracked under the pressure by now."

"Vivian Rothschild isn't most civilians," Harris reminded him with a thin smile. "Twenty-seven years with the Bureau teaches you a thing or two about maintaining cover."

Manny turned to Petrov. "And our internal situation?"

The Chief Security Officer straightened. "We observed Putu Amurao removing a package from the ship via the linen service truck this morning. My team followed at a distance. The package was delivered to Quinton Redmond at a café two kilometers from the port." A satisfied gleam appeared in his eyes. "Local authorities made the arrest quietly, and all stolen jewelry was recovered intact."

"Excellent work," Manny acknowledged. "And the third man? The spotter?"

"Still gathering conclusive evidence," Harris said, frustration briefly crossing her features. "We know his role is to identify passengers wearing valuable jewelry and relay that information to Desmond, who then coordinates the theft with Amurao. He's an accessory to all the crimes committed on this voyage, but we need positive identification before we move."

Manny's fingers drummed once on the table. "Where will the arrests take place? Here on the Aurelia or in Marseille?"

"Marseille," Marceau answered without hesitation. "French jurisdiction is preferable for prosecution, and we've coordinated with local authorities. The arrests will be discreet, away from the ship to minimize disruption to your operations and other passengers."

Manny nodded, satisfaction evident in the slight relaxation of his shoulders. "So, by tomorrow evening, this operation will conclude?"

"Barring unforeseen complications," Harris confirmed. "Once the arrests are made, we'll quietly notify the victims that their property has been recovered. Most passengers will never know what happened."

"And Captain Grimaldi?" Manny asked, his voice hardening slightly at the mention of his predecessor.

"Already in custody in Rome," Marceau replied. "The evidence against him is substantial. He won't be commanding another vessel."

Manny stood, signaling the end of the meeting. "Then we proceed as planned. By this time tomorrow, the Aurelia returns to what she does best, providing her passengers with memories worth treasuring, not investigations worth hiding."

The investigators gathered their materials as Manny walked to the window, gazing out at the sun beginning its descent toward the horizon. Tomorrow would bring resolution to this case, and perhaps clarity to his situation with Tessa. The thought brought a private smile to his face, invisible to the departing officers behind him.

Soon, he would be free to pursue what truly mattered. The Mediterranean stretched before him, golden in the evening light, full of possibilities yet to unfold.

* * *

Tessa slipped her key card into the door and pushed into her stateroom, dropping her shopping bags just inside the entrance. Her feet ached pleasantly from a day spent wandering Nice's sun-drenched streets, but it was the good kind of fatigue that comes with exploration and discovery.

She noticed the flowers immediately, a small but exquisite arrangement of Mediterranean blooms in vivid blues and whites nestled in a crystal vase. The card beside them bore the Selene Voyages emblem. Her fingers, suddenly not quite steady, plucked it from its envelope.

Tessa—Duty calls again tonight. I cannot join you for dinner, but would very much like to see you afterward. Our usual place at 10?—M

She traced the bold, confident handwriting with her fingertip. The man was becoming a delicious habit, one she wasn't sure she should indulge, and yet, the thought of not seeing him left an unexpected hollow in her evening plans.

Under the warm spray of the shower, Tessa let her thoughts drift through the peculiar events of the voyage: the lotharios, Richard's questionable activities, Gloria's illness, and the mysterious men who seemed to be following Richard. Something was coming to a head; she could feel it. Her lawyer's instinct for patterns and inconsistencies had never failed her, and it hummed now beneath her skin.

Yet as she toweled off and applied her favorite scented lotion, another thought emerged: maybe Manny would finally explain everything tonight. Maybe after Marseille, whatever had been claiming his attention would be resolved, leaving space for… what, exactly? She wasn't twenty-five anymore, ready to remake her life around a man. But at sixty-two, she wasn't done with possibility either.

The navy linen pants and flowing silk tunic she chose spoke of casual elegance, not effort. A single strand of pearls, her mother's. Simple gold hoops. No need to overthink this.

The Luna di Mare Lounge pulsed with soft jazz and gentle conversation when Tessa entered. She spotted Kelly and Liam immediately, their heads bent close together in what appeared to be an intense discussion. Kelly's hands gestured emphatically, her professional passion evident even from across the room. Liam's focus was complete, his expression thoughtful.

"… uses multi-layered neural networks that can identify cellular anomalies traditional pathology might miss," Kelly was saying as

Tessa approached. "The company's developing parallel treatment protocols based on genetic markers that…"

"Sorry to interrupt," Tessa said, sliding into the empty chair beside her daughter.

Kelly looked up, momentarily startled. "Mom! No, you're not interrupting. I was just explaining this incredible AI cancer diagnostics startup to Liam." She flashed a quick smile. "Turns out we have mutual professional interests after all."

"All fine," Liam added. "I've been picking your daughter's brain about venture capital strategies. My firm might be looking at similar opportunities."

A server appeared with menus, and Tessa ordered a glass of the Corsican white she'd grown fond of during the voyage.

"Where's the captain tonight?" Kelly asked, an eyebrow raised in gentle teasing.

"Unavailable for dinner," Tessa replied, keeping her tone light. "We're meeting for a nightcap later."

Julia and Seren arrived, dropping into the remaining chairs with the comfortable familiarity of old friends. Seren's bohemian caftan swirled around her as she settled, her silver bangles catching the lounge's muted lighting.

"I need sustenance and wine," Seren announced. "Nice completely wore me out today."

Julia laughed, already scanning the menu. "You? Exhausted? I thought you were indestructible."

"Even goddesses need rest," Seren quipped, then turned to Tessa. "Are you dining with the dashing captain tonight?"

"No, he had to cancel," Tessa said, feeling strangely protective of his absence. "But we're having drinks later."

"Mysterious man," Julia mused. "I wonder what keeps him so busy."

"Running a ship this size is no small task," Liam offered.

Kelly straightened slightly. "Do you think it has anything to do with Richard Collier? That man following him today was definitely security of some kind."

"I'd bet money on it," Seren said, leaning forward conspiratorially. "Three husbands taught me one valuable lesson: when men are evasive, there's always a reason."

"Not necessarily a nefarious one," Julia countered. "Sometimes it's just… complicated."

* * *

"Something interesting happening over there?" Julia asked, following Tessa's gaze across the lounge.

As if on cue, Patrick Desmond and Vivian Rothschild entered the lounge, making their way through the scattered tables with practiced elegance. Patrick's hand rested lightly at the small of Vivian's back, guiding her toward a semi-secluded spot near the windows. His smile carried the confident assurance of a man who believed himself irresistible.

"Speak of the devil," Seren murmured, watching them settle in.

Kelly leaned closer to the group. "That's one of them, right? The lotharios you've been tracking?"

"Patrick Desmond," Tessa confirmed, keeping her voice low. "And that's Vivian Rothschild with him; one of the diamond-level guests."

They watched as Patrick signaled a server, who approached with the deference reserved for high-spending guests. "Martini, very dry," he ordered, then turned to Vivian with exaggerated attentiveness.

Vivian made a point of smiling at the server. "My usual, please," she said, her diamond bracelet catching the light as she gestured.

"Of course, Ms. Rothschild," the server confirmed.

Tessa tried to curb her curiosity and focus on her friends, but found her attention drifting back to the couple by the window. Patrick had leaned in, his expression animated, hands moving with convincing enthusiasm. Despite herself, Tessa strained to catch snippets of their conversation.

"… absolute certainty," Patrick was saying, his voice carrying just enough for Tessa to hear. "You're making a fabulous investment."

Vivian nodded, her expression carefully measured between interest and caution.

"Double your money in just a few months," Patrick continued, his voice dropping again before rising with another burst of enthusiasm. "The technology is revolutionary."

Liam's eyebrows rose slightly as he, too, caught Patrick's words. He and Kelly exchanged a meaningful glance.

"I can't understand why you couldn't initiate the wire from your computer," Patrick said, a note of impatience barely concealed beneath his charm. "The banking app is perfectly secure."

Vivian's laugh tinkled like expensive crystal. "Oh, Patrick. I'm just a simple woman who prefers doing important business face-to-face." She patted his hand indulgently. "I'm not comfortable making such a large transfer from a computer."

"But it would be so much more convenient…"

"Besides," Vivian cut him off gently, "it will only take a little while, and after, we can have a wonderful lunch in Marseille. I know the most divine little restaurant near the Vieux Port."

Patrick's smile returned, though something calculating flickered behind his eyes. "Of course. Whatever makes you comfortable."

"Tessa?" Seren called, then repeated more loudly, "Tessa!"

Tessa startled, turning back to find all four of her companions staring at her. "I'm sorry, what?"

"You were miles away," Seren said with a knowing smile. "Or rather, about twenty feet away, eavesdropping."

"I wasn't…" Tessa began, then shrugged with a small laugh. "Alright, I was."

"Anything interesting?" Julia asked quietly.

"He's pressuring her to wire money for some investment." Tessa glanced back at Patrick and Vivian. "She's insisting on doing it in person at a bank in Marseille."

"Smart woman," Kelly commented. "Though if it's one of those fake AI startups I've been hearing about lately, she's still being conned. The tech sector is crawling with those scams right now."

"Well," Seren announced, standing up with a dramatic flourish of her caftan, "as fascinating as this real-time crime drama is, I'm starving. We're going to dinner."

"Agreed," Julia said, gathering her things. "Intrigue is much better enjoyed on a full stomach."

Liam rose smoothly. "The Trattoria has a wonderful ravioli special tonight. Miguel mentioned it earlier."

As they made their way out of the lounge, Tessa cast one final glance toward Patrick and Vivian. The woman's composure was remarkable; either Patrick's charm completely took her in, or she was playing a very sophisticated game of her own. Either way, Tessa couldn't shake the feeling that whatever was unfolding would come to a head soon.

Chapter 15

The Selene Voyages, Aurelia settled into its berth at Port Vendres, France, during the predawn period, its immense ivory-colored form shimmering in contrast to the quaint scenic marina. The heavens were slowly shifting from a deep purple hue to the soft amber of daybreak while the vessel's personnel readied themselves for the upcoming day's shore expeditions.

Below deck, in the sterile confines of the chief security officer's office, Manny paced with measured steps. This was an unusual place to find the captain, but today was different.

"They're beginning disembarkation now, Captain," Petrov reported, his eyes fixed on security monitors showing streams of passengers filing down the gangways.

Manny nodded, his silver hair catching the fluorescent light. "And our persons of interest?"

"All still on board. Rothschild and Desmond are scheduled for the 9:30 excursion to Marseille. Collier is booked for a private tour at 10:00." Petrov's voice remained professionally detached, though tension crept around his eyes. "The third suspect appears to be having breakfast on Deck 8."

In another part of the ship, three decks below, a junior security officer in plain clothes monitored the Housekeeping Manager Putu Amurao, who was moving through the crew areas with practiced efficiency. Amurao paused occasionally to check his own phone, his movements growing increasingly agitated with each passing minute.

Back in Petrov's office, the chief security officer and Manny watched as the pier gradually cleared. Tour buses departed in orderly succession, taxis pulled away with smaller groups of passengers, and the initial rush thinned to a trickle.

"Now," Manny said quietly.

Petrov's fingers moved across his phone, sending a series of precisely worded text messages. Within minutes, an unmarked black sedan and a police vehicle with French insignia pulled alongside the ship, parking in a restricted area near the cargo access point.

Four individuals emerged: two uniformed police officers and two plainclothes agents, one sporting the unmistakable bearing of law enforcement despite her civilian attire. They moved with quiet purpose, presenting credentials to the security personnel at the base of the cargo gangway.

"Agents coming aboard, Captain," one of Petrov's officers reported through the secure radio.

Manny straightened his uniform jacket, his face settling into lines of grim determination. "Show them directly to this office. And have someone bring Amurao here. Use the housekeeping issue we discussed."

"Yes, sir."

A sharp knock preceded the arrival of the law enforcement team. Introductions were brief and professional; everyone understood what was at stake.

"Manager Amurao is approaching," Petrov's radio crackled.

Another knock, softer this time. Putu Amurao entered, his expression shifting from professional concern to shock as he registered the presence of police officers and plainclothes agents.

"Mr. Amurao," the female Interpol agent began, her voice steady and formal, "I am Agent Ferreira with Interpol. We are placing you under arrest for your involvement in multiple thefts of valuable jewelry from passenger staterooms aboard this vessel."

The color drained from Amurao's face. His eyes darted to Manny, who returned his gaze with steely disappointment.

"You have the right to remain silent," one of the French officers continued, stepping forward with handcuffs. "Anything you say…"

"This is a mistake," Amurao interrupted, his voice cracking. "Captain, there must be some misunderstanding!"

"We have video footage of you removing stolen items from the ship and delivering them to your fence," Manny replied, his tone flat. "The evidence is conclusive, Mr. Amurao."

The realization that there was no escape path visibly settled over the housekeeping manager. His shoulders slumped as the handcuffs clicked into place.

The officers escorted Amurao from the office, moving efficiently toward the gangway where they would transfer him to the waiting police vehicle, away from the main passenger areas to avoid creating a scene.

"Phase one complete," Petrov said quietly, checking his phone for updates from the agents tracking Desmond and Collier in Marseille. "Now we wait."

Manny nodded, moving to the window that overlooked the sparkling Mediterranean. "And hope the rest of the operation unfolds as planned."

The next phase of the operation unfolded with the precision of a Swiss timepiece. In the heart of Marseille, the bank that Vivian had selected stood inconspicuous among the city's blend of historic and modern architecture. Inside, an Interpol agent posing as a loan officer shuffled papers at his desk, while outside, two more agents browsed their phones on a nearby bench, their casual demeanor belying their vigilance.

Agent Marceau and Diane Harris sat in an unmarked Peugeot across the street, windows slightly cracked despite the air conditioning. Marceau checked his earpiece while Harris monitored the tablet displaying feeds from cameras strategically positioned around the bank.

"Target approaching from the east," came a voice through their earpieces. "Desmond and Rothschild on foot, approximately fifty meters out."

Harris tapped her screen, switching to a street view. "Visual confirmed. Operation is a go."

Through the camera feed, they watched Patrick and Vivian strolling toward the bank. Patrick walked with the confident swagger of a man who believed victory was within his grasp. Beside him, Vivian played her part flawlessly; her diamond rings catching the sunlight, her designer handbag swinging gently as she chatted animatedly about potential returns on her investment.

"She's good," Harris murmured appreciatively.

"Twenty-seven years with the Bureau," Marceau replied. "Old habits die hard."

Inside the bank, the undercover manager straightened his tie as the alert came through his earpiece. The trap was set, the players in position. When Patrick and Vivian pushed through the glass doors, he greeted them with practiced courtesy.

"Bonjour, Madame, Monsieur. How may I assist you today?"

Vivian offered a warm smile. "I'd like to make a wire transfer, please. Quite a substantial one."

"Of course. Please, follow me to my office, where we can handle this privately."

Patrick placed his hand on Vivian's lower back, guiding her forward, a gesture of intimacy that made Marceau's jaw tighten as he watched on the monitor. The three disappeared into a private office with frosted glass walls.

Inside, Vivian settled into a leather chair, removing her designer sunglasses and placing them carefully in her purse. "I wish to transfer two hundred fifty thousand dollars to an investment account," she announced, her voice carrying the precise blend of excitement and nervousness one would expect from a wealthy widow making a significant financial move.

Patrick leaned forward eagerly. "I have all the routing information right here." He produced a folded paper from his breast pocket, sliding it across the polished desk.

The bank manager examined the document with professional detachment, though his trained eye immediately recognized the offshore account structure commonly used in financial fraud schemes. "Everything appears in order, Madame. I'll need you to complete some forms, and we can process this immediately."

The paperwork took only minutes. Patrick grew increasingly animated as the transaction progressed, checking his phone repeatedly. When the confirmation came through that the wire had been received, a smile spread across his face.

"There we are, Madame Rothschild," the manager said, printing a receipt with a flourish. "Your transfer is complete."

"Oh, I must have that receipt," Vivian said, reaching for the paper. "I'm terribly old-fashioned about these things. Can't trust computers, you know. I like paper evidence of my transactions."

Patrick chuckled indulgently. "Soon enough, you'll have much better evidence when your investment doubles."

They rose to leave, Patrick already talking about a celebratory lunch at a nearby bistro. As they approached the bank's entrance, Vivian touched his arm.

"Patrick, darling, would you excuse me for just a moment? I need to use the ladies' room before our lunch."

"Of course," he agreed, watching as she disappeared down a side hallway.

The bank manager approached Patrick almost immediately. "Monsieur Desmond? I'm terribly sorry to bother you, but there seems to be a small discrepancy with the transfer. Nothing serious, just a formality with the routing number. Could you step back to my office for a moment? It won't take long."

Confusion flickered across Patrick's face. "A problem? But I received confirmation."

"Just a technical matter. We can resolve it in moments."

As Patrick reluctantly followed the manager back toward the office, two men in business casual attire entered the bank, moving with purposeful strides. Outside, the unmarked Peugeot pulled up to the curb, joined seconds later by a police vehicle with subdued lights.

Inside the manager's office, Patrick's confusion turned to alarm as the door opened to reveal the two men who had entered the bank. They were no longer maintaining their casual demeanor.

"Patrick Desmond," one said, producing identification. "I am Agent Bélanger with Interpol. You are under arrest for wire fraud, conspiracy, and theft."

Patrick's face drained of color. "There must be some mistake…"

"There is no mistake, Monsieur Desmond," the agent replied, producing handcuffs.

As they led him through the bank, Patrick's eyes darted frantically, searching for Vivian. Instead, he spotted her outside through the glass doors, standing calmly beside the unmarked Peugeot. She was speaking to Agent Marceau and Diane Harris with the composed professionalism of a colleague, not the nervous excitement of a mark.

The realization hit him like a physical blow. Vivian had never been his target; he had been hers all along.

* * *

In another part of Marseille, two plainclothes Interpol agents maintained their positions at separate tables of a small café on Rue de la République. Agent Klaus Weber sipped his espresso methodically, scrolling through his phone. His attention never truly left the two men seated across the narrow cobblestone street.

Richard Collier and Emil Kuester, the third lothario from the Aurelia, were sharing a carafe of wine despite the early hour. Their postures suggested casual conversation, but Weber noted the telltale signs of anxiety: Collier's frequent glance at his watch, Kuester's nervous scanning of passing pedestrians. They appeared to be waiting for someone, almost certainly the fence who was supposed to buy the stolen jewelry from the ship.

What they didn't know was that their contact, Quinton Redmond, had been quietly arrested in Nice the previous day, and the jewelry had been recovered from his hotel room safe.

Agent Weber's phone vibrated silently against the café table. A simple text message: "Green light." He caught the eye of his colleague, Agent Sophie Dubois, positioned at a corner table with a perfect view of the street. She acknowledged with an imperceptible nod.

Both agents rose casually, leaving payment beneath their saucers. As they did, two unmarked police vehicles rolled to a stop at either end of the narrow street, effectively blocking any potential escape route.

Weber approached from behind Collier while Dubois positioned herself behind Kuester. Neither man noticed the agents until they were directly behind them, their attention fixed on the approaching police officers emerging from the vehicles.

"Excuse me," a portly Frenchman at a neighboring table called out loudly in accented English. "I believe those officers are coming for you."

Richard Collier turned sharply, his expression morphing from confusion to shock as he found himself staring directly at Agent Weber's Interpol credentials.

"Richard Collier, also known as Thomas Evans," Weber stated calmly, his voice carrying just enough authority to freeze Collier mid-rise. One large hand came to rest firmly on Collier's shoulder, applying gentle but unmistakable pressure. "Please remain seated."

Across the table, Emil Kuester sat motionless, his face drained of color as Agent Dubois presented her credentials.

"Gentlemen, you are being detained on suspicion of fraud, theft, and criminal conspiracy," Weber continued, his accent clipping the words precisely.

The café had fallen silent, other patrons watching the scene unfold with expressions ranging from alarm to the particular delight the French take in unexpected street theater. A waiter froze in place; a tray of pastries suspended in mid-air.

"This is ridiculous," Collier attempted, his New England accent thickening with stress. "There's been some mistake…"

"No mistake, Mr. Collier," Dubois interjected smoothly. "We have documented your transfer of funds from Gloria Sullivan's account yesterday. The account you transferred to, under the name Thomas Evans, has been frozen."

Kuester remained silent, seeming to shrink into himself as uniformed officers approached, handcuffs ready.

Within moments, both men were being escorted to separate police vehicles, their protests fading as the reality of their situation became clear. The café erupted in excited chatter as the cars pulled away, already transforming the arrest into the day's most thrilling anecdote.

Weber and Dubois walked unhurriedly toward their own vehicle, where they reported the successful completion of their phase of the operation.

As they drove toward police headquarters, Weber's phone pinged with confirmation; Patrick Desmond had been successfully apprehended at the bank. The operation had proceeded exactly as planned.

Miles away, aboard the Aurelia, Captain Manny Delgado would soon receive word that all targets had been neutralized. By evening, the Aurelia would sail with four fewer passengers than it had arrived with, and with its reputation and the safety of its guests secured once more.

The Mediterranean sparkled beneath the midday sun, indifferent to the human drama playing out along its ancient shores. Justice, like the tide, had its own rhythm and timing, sometimes slow, sometimes swift, but ultimately inevitable.

Chapter 16

The morning sun bathed Marseille in a golden glow as the circle of five stepped from their private Mercedes van onto the cobblestones near Vieux-Port. The harbor stretched before them—a forest of white masts bobbing against the backdrop of limestone hills and the imposing silhouette of Notre-Dame de la Garde basilica perched high above the city.

"Thank you for arranging yet another fantastic day," Julia said, adjusting her wide-brimmed hat against the Mediterranean glare.

Seren shrugged with practiced nonchalance. "Jean-Pierre's been my driver for years whenever I'm in Marseille. His grandfather was a fisherman here; he knows every secret corner of this city."

Jean-Pierre, a silver-haired man with sun-weathered skin and keen eyes, closed the van door and gestured toward the harbor. "We begin with morning coffee at the port, non? Then perhaps the basilica for the views before the crowds arrive."

The group followed their guide through the morning bustle of the harbor, weaving between fishmongers arranging their catches and locals selecting the freshest sea bass and bream. The scent of salt air mingled with fresh coffee as they settled at a small café terrace.

By mid-morning, they had ascended to Notre-Dame de la Garde, where the sprawling panorama of Marseille unfolded beneath them: terracotta rooftops, limestone cliffs, and the impossibly blue Mediterranean stretching to the horizon.

"I do not do justice to this view with my cell phone camera," Julia murmured, her writer's eye cataloging the play of light and shadow.

After lingering over the basilica's Byzantine mosaics, Jean-Pierre drove them to Le Panier district, Marseille's oldest neighborhood. Here, narrow streets climbed steeply between pastel-colored buildings, vibrant street art adorned weathered walls, and tiny shops displayed their wares on the sidewalks.

"We meet at Place de Lenche in three hours," Jean-Pierre instructed. "Take your time. Get lost a little; it's the only way to truly see Le Panier."

The friends split into natural pairs—Julia and Seren heading toward a colorful spice shop, while Liam was drawn to a tiny bookstore. Tessa and Kelly wandered together, their pace unhurried as they explored the labyrinthine streets.

They turned a corner onto a narrow lane where boutiques displayed handcrafted jewelry and clothing. Kelly stopped abruptly, her attention caught by a small atelier window. Behind the glass hung a simple, elegant gown of ivory silk, minimalist in design but with exquisite draping that spoke of masterful craftsmanship.

"It's beautiful," Tessa said, following her daughter's gaze.

Kelly nodded, a soft smile playing at her lips. "It reminds me of something Briana sketched once."

"Will you wear a gown for the wedding?" Tessa asked, her voice careful, neutral. "Or will Briana? Or both of you?"

Kelly turned to her mother, amusement lighting her eyes. "Mom, there's no rulebook for this. That's what's kind of wonderful about it."

"I know, I just…" Tessa shook her head. "I'm still learning the etiquette."

"There is no etiquette," Kelly laughed. "That's the point. We decide what feels right for us." She glanced back at the dress. "We've talked about it. Briana loves the idea of both of us in dresses, but in different styles that reflect our personalities. I'm leaning toward a tailored suit, though."

Tessa squeezed her daughter's hand. "Whatever you choose, you'll both be beautiful."

They reunited with the others at a sun-drenched restaurant in the Place de Lenche, where tables spilled across the ancient square. The waiter brought platters of bouillabaisse, Marseille's famed fish stew, its saffron-orange broth rich with local seafood.

"I haven't seen a single lothario all day," Tessa remarked, breaking off a piece of crusty bread. "No Vivian, no Patrick Desmond."

"No Richard Collier either," Seren added, reaching for her wine. "Perhaps they've all found greener pastures."

Julia raised an eyebrow. "Or they're plotting something particularly nefarious."

"Any updates from your inside source?" Kelly asked Liam.

Liam shook his head. "I haven't spoken to Miguel today. He works late, so he wasn't up before we left."

"I still say they're running a con," Seren declared. "The classic honeytrap: seduce the wealthy widows, then vanish with their jewelry and bank accounts."

"But why involve the captain?" Julia wondered. "That's the piece I can't fit."

Tessa frowned slightly, remembering Manny's promise that everything would make sense soon. "Perhaps we're missing something."

Their speculation was interrupted by the arrival of a basket of fresh figs and local cheeses. The conversation drifted to lighter topics: the architecture they'd admired, the tiny shop where Seren found hand-painted ceramics, the elderly man who'd shown Julia his collection of vintage maps.

As they lingered over dessert, the Mediterranean breeze carrying the scent of lavender from a nearby stall, Tessa found herself hoping that whatever storm had been brewing aboard the Aurelia had passed. For now, surrounded by friends and her daughter in this ancient, sun-washed city, the mysteries of the ship seemed distant and unimportant.

"To Marseille," Liam proposed, raising his glass.

* * *

The afternoon sun cast a golden glow over Marseille as the group made their way through the MuCEM's striking latticed exterior. Inside, the Museum of European and Mediterranean Civilizations offered a cool respite from the heat, its exhibits tracing the rich cultural tapestry of the region through artifacts, art, and interactive displays.

"I could spend days here," Julia remarked, notebook in hand as she jotted impressions of a particularly moving installation on migration patterns across the Mediterranean.

Seren drifted toward an exhibit on traditional healing practices, her eyes lighting up at the display of ancient herbal remedies. "Some of these plants I use in my homemade remedies," she explained to Liam, who listened with genuine interest.

Kelly and Tessa moved through the galleries together, their shared experience in Marseille having somehow deepened their connection beyond the revelation of the previous night. They paused before a collection of family photographs spanning generations of Mediterranean life.

"Strange how some things are universal," Kelly observed. "Look at the way that grandmother is looking at her granddaughter; it's exactly how Grandma looked at me when I was little."

Tessa smiled, touched by the observation. "Some things transcend time and place."

After the museum, Jean-Pierre drove them to Cours Julien, a bohemian neighborhood alive with street art and independent boutiques. The women scattered among the shops while Liam found a café table and ordered espresso, content to people-watch in the afternoon sun.

Seren emerged triumphant from a tiny boutique with packages of lavender sachets and hand-milled soaps. "For Briana," she announced to Kelly, presenting her with a small gift bag. "A little something from her Aunty Seren."

As the sun began its descent, painting Marseille's limestone buildings in warm amber light, they gathered their purchases and headed back to Jean-Pierre's waiting vehicle.

"Just think," Kelly mused as they wound through the city streets toward the port, "we only have one more port day before the cruise ends." She leaned her head against the window, watching the scenery pass. "I've had such an amazing time, seeing all these incredible places, meeting Liam," she smiled across at him, "and watching an international mystery unfold right before our eyes. It's been better than any vacation I could have imagined."

"But?" Tessa prompted, hearing the undercurrent in her daughter's voice.

Kelly smiled. "But I'm ready to get home to Briana. Start planning our life together. The wedding."

"I know exactly what you mean," Tessa said softly. "Though I have to say how happy I am that you surprised me by coming along. Having you here has made everything so much more special."

Kelly reached across and squeezed her mother's hand. "Even with all the drama?"

"Especially with all the drama," Tessa laughed.

As Jean-Pierre pulled up to the cruise terminal, the massive white hull of the Aurelia looming above them, Julia suddenly straightened in her seat.

"Look there," she said, pointing toward the rear gangway, a separate entrance from the main one that most passengers used. "Isn't that Vivian?"

They all turned to see Vivian Rothschild, elegant even in casual travel clothes, walking down the gangway, accompanied by a man and a younger woman, both carrying small pieces of luggage. A black sedan with tinted windows waited at the bottom.

"That's them," Tessa said, recognition dawning. "The two people who were following Richard yesterday in Nice." She narrowed her eyes, watching as Vivian spoke briefly with the pair before all three climbed into the waiting car. "Why would she be leaving with them? Unless…"

"Unless she's somehow involved," Liam finished, his expression thoughtful.

"But involved how?" Kelly asked. "Is she another victim, or…"

"Or is she working with them?" Julia suggested.

Seren shook her head, bracelets jingling softly. "The plot thickens, my dears."

The black sedan pulled away, disappearing into the flow of port traffic, taking with it any immediate answers to their questions.

"Come on," Tessa said finally, gathering her shopping bags. "I think it's time we got back on board. Something tells me there are more pieces to this puzzle than we realized."

* * *

The quintet joined the flow of passengers returning to the ship, each person in their own world of thought as they filtered through security. Seren chattered with the crew member scanning her cruise card, asking about his day as though they were old friends. Julia retrieved her camera from her bag, eager to download the day's photos before they slipped from memory. Kelly's thumbs flew across her phone screen, updating Briana on their unexpected crime drama sighting, while Liam walked with hands in pockets, whistling softly.

Tessa followed behind, thoughts swirling around Manny and what role, if any, he played in today's events. Was he involved? A victim? Part of the solution?

"Meet in the Aureate Lounge at seven?" Seren called as they reached the bank of elevators.

Everyone nodded agreement before dispersing to their respective decks, the day's discoveries hanging between them like an unfinished conversation.

When Tessa unlocked her suite door, she immediately noticed the silver ice bucket on her coffee table. A bottle of Veuve Clicquot rested inside, beaded with condensation, alongside a cream-colored envelope bearing her name in a strong, masculine script.

She kicked off her sandals and sank onto the sofa, slipping her finger beneath the envelope flap.

Tessa,

Today marks the end of a difficult operation and the beginning of what I hope will be something beautiful. Join me for dinner in my quarters at 8:00? The mysteries I've been unable to share will finally be revealed.

Yours,

Manny

Tessa pressed the note to her chest, a small smile playing at her lips. After the odd events of recent days, clarity beckoned like a lighthouse.

She drew a bath, adding lavender oil from the ship's luxury amenities collection. Steam rose around her as she lowered herself into the water, tension melting from her shoulders. Her mind drifted between the events they'd witnessed and the promise of Manny's invitation.

After her bath, Tessa stood before her closet, fingertips trailing across the hanging garments. She bypassed her usual dinner choices, selecting instead a midnight blue silk dress she'd brought on impulse. Its draped neckline revealed just enough collarbone to be intriguing without crossing into inappropriate, while the bias cut skimmed her curves with elegant simplicity.

She twisted her hair into a loose chignon, allowing a few silver strands to escape and frame her face. A touch of mascara, a subtle smoky eye, and a swipe of her favorite burgundy lipstick completed the effect. Around her neck, she clasped a simple silver pendant, a gift from Kelly years ago.

Tessa slipped into strappy silver sandals with just enough heel to give her confidence without sacrificing comfort. A spritz of perfume at her wrists and neck, one last glance in the mirror, and she was ready.

At precisely 7:00, Tessa entered the Aureate Lounge to find the others already gathered around their usual table. Julia spotted her first, eyebrows rising in appreciation.

"Well, look at you," Seren exclaimed, eyes twinkling. "Someone's dressed for more than just dinner."

Tessa felt heat rising to her cheeks. "Manny invited me to his quarters. He left champagne and a note saying today's a day to celebrate."

"I'd say so," Kelly agreed, giving her mother an appraising once-over. "That color is amazing on you."

"The captain's a lucky man," Julia added with a gentle smile.

Liam signaled the waiter for another round before leaning in conspiratorially. "I spoke with Miguel earlier. He says the

Housekeeping Manager was arrested and escorted off the ship this morning."

"Arrested?" Tessa echoed.

Liam nodded. "And three passengers disembarked with their luggage, but not through the main gangway. They were accompanied by security. Three others never returned to the ship."

"Six?" Kelly frowned. "We only saw Vivian and those two agents. That means…"

"Richard and his friend were probably two of the others," Julia reasoned.

"And Patrick," Seren finished.

They exchanged knowing glances, pieces falling into place.

"It seems our little band of amateur detectives was onto something after all," Julia said.

Tessa checked her watch. "I should go. Manny promised explanations, and I intend to collect."

Kelly caught her mother's arm as she stood. "Just remember," she said, eyes dancing with mischief, "no walks of shame down the corridor tomorrow morning. Those security cameras see everything."

"Kelly!" Tessa protested, but couldn't help laughing. "I'm a grown woman, you know."

"Don't I know it." Kelly grinned. "Just looking out for your reputation, Counselor."

Tessa squeezed her daughter's shoulder. "I'll remember that when you bring Briana to meet me."

With a final wave, Tessa headed for the elevator, heart quickening with each step toward Manny's quarters and whatever revelations awaited her there.

Chapter 17

As Tessa approached the Captain's quarters, she found herself smoothing her dress with slightly trembling hands. She took a deep breath, steadying herself before continuing down the corridor.

Outside Manny's door stood a uniformed butler, who greeted her with a respectful nod. He gave a gentle knock before opening the door and announcing her arrival with practiced formality.

"Ms. Monroe, Captain."

The Captain's quarters were even more impressive than Tessa had imagined. Lustrous wood paneling, nautical art that managed to be tasteful rather than kitschy, and expansive windows that showcased the darkening Mediterranean sky. Through the open balcony doors, Tessa could see Manny's silhouette against the twilight.

He turned at her entrance, and Tessa felt a flutter in her chest. The transformation was remarkable; the weight that had visibly burdened him for days had lifted. His face was relaxed, his shoulders no longer rigid with tension. This was the Manny she'd first met aboard the Iridessa, confident and at ease with his command.

"Tessa," he breathed, crossing the room to greet her. His eyes traveled appreciatively from her face to her dress and back again. "You look absolutely stunning. That color…" He shook his head slightly, as if words failed him.

"Thank you," she replied, pleased by his reaction. "You look rather unburdened yourself."

Manny smiled, the lines around his eyes crinkling. "That I am. Finally."

With a small nod to the butler, Manny indicated it was time for drinks. The man moved smoothly to a silver tray where a bottle of champagne waited in an ice bucket. He poured two flutes with practiced precision.

"We are ready to begin dinner service," Manny instructed, accepting the glasses and handing one to Tessa.

"Of course, Captain," the butler replied before discreetly withdrawing.

Manny gestured toward the balcony. "Shall we?"

Outside, Tessa discovered an intimate dining setup that rivaled any five-star restaurant. A small table draped in crisp white linen stood ready, silver gleaming in the soft lighting from hurricane lamps. The balcony itself was spacious enough to feel luxurious without losing its intimate atmosphere.

"I hope you don't mind dining in tonight," Manny said, pulling out her chair. "I thought we might appreciate some privacy for our conversation."

"It's perfect," Tessa assured him, settling into her seat. The gentle breeze carried the scent of the sea, and stars were beginning to appear in the darkening sky.

Manny took his place across from her, raising his glass. "To patience. Thank you for yours this past week. Things have been…" he paused, searching for the right word, "quite unusual."

"That's putting it mildly," Tessa replied with a small smile, touching her glass to his.

"I promise to tell you everything over dinner," he said, his expression turning earnest. "But first, I want to hear about your day in Marseille. Did you enjoy yourself despite the drama?"

Tessa took a sip of champagne. "It was certainly memorable. The Old Port was beautiful, and we had lunch at the most charming restaurant overlooking the harbor."

"La Perle, perhaps?" Manny asked, his eyes twinkling with something like foreknowledge.

"As a matter of fact, yes. How did you…"

Their conversation was gently interrupted by the butler's return, bearing two exquisite plates of seafood appetizers garnished with microgreens and edible flowers.

"Your first course, Captain, Madam," he announced, placing the dishes before them with practiced grace.

As the butler retreated, Tessa caught Manny's gaze across the candlelight, both of them aware that the moment for revelations was finally at hand.

* * *

The candlelight cast a warm glow on Manny's face as he swirled the last of his wine before setting the glass down. The captain had a natural storyteller's cadence, his Italian accent deepening as he leaned forward across the table toward Tessa.

"I first must apologize for my… how do you say… evasiveness," he began. "When Selene Voyages asked me to step in for Captain Grimaldi, they were not entirely forthcoming about why."

Tessa nodded, her fork poised over her plate. "I suspected there was more happening than you could say."

"There was." Manny's expression turned serious. "About three months ago, a woman who had sailed on the Aurelia filed a complaint. She had been conned by a man she met on board, a considerable sum. When security investigated, they discovered something troubling."

"The thefts," Tessa supplied.

Manny's eyebrows lifted slightly. "You pieced some of this together, no?"

"We noticed certain patterns," she admitted. "The men who seemed to target wealthy single women, the missing jewelry…"

"You are observant as you are beautiful," he said. "Yes, there were several thefts, particularly of jewelry, on the Aurelia. More than what we would consider normal."

"Normal?" Tessa's brow furrowed. "You expect theft on these cruises?"

Manny spread his hands in a gesture of regret. "Unfortunately, where there are valuables, there will sometimes be those who covet them. Usually, these are isolated incidents. But on the Aurelia, the pattern was too consistent to ignore."

The butler silently appeared with a bottle of white wine, pouring with practiced precision before disappearing again.

"The FBI became involved first," Manny continued, "because many of the victims were American citizens. But as the investigation expanded, they discovered these thefts crossed international boundaries."

"Interpol," Tessa said, connecting the dots.

"Exactly. Together, they uncovered a sophisticated operation, a ring of men who sailed luxury cruise lines, including Selene Voyages. These men offered companionship to single, wealthy women while simultaneously running confidence schemes and orchestrating jewelry thefts."

The Mediterranean breeze lifted the edges of the tablecloth as Manny leaned back in his chair, his expression darkening.

"They worked in teams of three or four. One would identify targets wearing valuable jewelry and relay the information. Another would charm the women, sometimes convincing them to invest in fictitious opportunities. Meanwhile, someone would gain access to their cabins and steal the jewelry."

Tessa's mind raced, putting together all the observations they'd made over the voyage. "Richard Collier, Patrick Desmond…"

"Part of the same ring, yes," Manny confirmed. "But what made this case particularly troubling was the discovery that they had help from inside the Aurelia." His jaw tightened. "Captain Grimaldi was facilitating their activities."

"The captain himself?" Tessa couldn't hide her shock. "But why would he risk his career, his reputation…?"

"Money," Manny said simply. "He was taking kickbacks from these men. For each wealthy woman he introduced them to, for each theft he helped facilitate, he received a percentage."

Tessa set down her fork, appetite momentarily forgotten. "That's why you stepped in when Gloria fell ill."

"I knew something was wrong," Manny acknowledged. "The investigation had already determined that Richard drugged other women to gain access to their financial information. When Gloria didn't return to the ship, I insisted we wait."

The butler appeared again, this time to clear their first course plates. Tessa observed how Manny immediately shifted his demeanor, smiling politely at the crew member, maintaining the pleasant façade of a captain hosting a guest. Only when the butler was gone did his expression grow serious again.

"So Patrick Desmond, Richard Collier, and the others, they're all part of this criminal organization?" Tessa asked as the butler returned, setting down their second course with a flourish.

"Thank you," Manny said to the butler. "This looks wonderful."

The plates before them featured delicate filets of sea bass atop a bright saffron risotto, surrounded by a scattering of mussels and clams in their shells. The aroma was intoxicating: herbs, butter, the essence of the Mediterranean itself.

The butler bowed slightly. "Would Madam prefer more wine?"

Tessa shook her head. "This is perfect, thank you."

As the butler retreated, Manny continued the explanation he'd begun, his voice growing more serious. "Yes, Richard and Patrick were part of the same criminal organization. The third man, the one your friend Liam noticed watching Richard in Nice, was their spotter. His job was to identify wealthy passengers wearing valuable jewelry and relay that information back to Patrick."

Tessa nodded, taking a sip of wine as pieces of the puzzle clicked into place. "And the housekeeping manager was involved, too?"

"Unfortunately, yes. Putu Amurao was their inside man. He provided access to staterooms when passengers were ashore." Manny's expression darkened. "He was detained this morning. It's always difficult when crew members betray the trust we place in them."

"How extensive was this operation?" Tessa asked, setting down her fork.

"Larger than we initially thought. Captain Grimaldi was involved from the beginning, making introductions between the lotharios and wealthy single women, looking the other way when thefts occurred, even taking a percentage of their profits." Manny shook his head in disgust. "The investigation has linked them to similar schemes on other cruise lines across the Mediterranean and Caribbean."

The golden light from the hurricane lamps caught in Tessa's eyes as she processed this information. "And Vivian? I saw her leaving the ship with her luggage this afternoon, accompanied by a man and woman."

A smile tugged at Manny's lips. "Ah, Vivian. She's quite remarkable. She's actually a retired FBI agent."

"A what?" Tessa's eyebrows shot up in surprise.

"Her sister was victimized by a similar scheme last year, lost nearly half a million dollars to a man she met on a cruise. When the FBI and Interpol were planning this operation, Vivian volunteered. She was never in any danger," Manny assured her. "Agent Diane Harris from the FBI and Agent Marceau from Interpol were on board the entire time, monitoring the situation."

Tessa sat back in her chair, memories of Vivian's confident demeanor taking on new meaning. "So that's why she seemed so at ease with Patrick. I worried she was being taken advantage of."

"She played her role perfectly," Manny confirmed. "And the man and woman you saw her leaving with were Harris and Marceau. Their work here is complete."

The butler silently appeared to clear their plates and present the main course, a delicate seafood risotto studded with saffron and tender morsels of lobster. The aroma was intoxicating, but Tessa found herself more captivated by the revelations than the food.

"And your role in all this?" she asked once they were alone again.

Manny's fingers brushed against the stem of his wine glass. "When Selene Voyages discovered Grimaldi's involvement, they needed someone they trusted to step in discreetly. I was asked to facilitate the operation, particularly to arrange the introduction between Vivian and Patrick, who Interpol believes is the ringleader."

"That's what I overheard that day," Tessa said, understanding dawning. "You weren't setting up a wealthy passenger; you were positioning an undercover agent."

"Exactly." Manny's eyes met hers across the table. "I couldn't tell you then. The operation depended on absolute secrecy."

Tessa felt a flush of embarrassment warm her cheeks. "I feel foolish now. I saw you with Patrick, remembered similar men operating on the Iridessa, and jumped to conclusions."

"Don't." Manny reached across the table, his hand covering hers. The warmth of his touch sent a pleasant tingle up her arm. "Your suspicions were perfectly reasonable given what you observed. In fact, your instincts about these men were correct from the beginning."

The evening breeze carried the distant sounds of music from somewhere below deck, a gentle melody that seemed to underscore the moment. Tessa turned her hand beneath his, their fingers intertwining naturally.

"When I first spotted you boarding in Valletta," Manny continued, his voice softening, "I worried this assignment might complicate things between us. The timing seemed almost cruel."

"And now?" Tessa asked, suddenly aware of how close their faces had grown as they leaned toward each other across the table.

Manny's eyes held hers, sincere and warm. "Now I'm wondering if we can move forward, Tessa. Get to know each other properly, without international intrigue getting in the way." His lips curved into a smile. "Unless you find that sort of thing appealing, of course."

Tessa laughed, the sound clear and genuine. "I think I've had enough intrigue for one cruise. Though I must admit, watching you command a situation has its appeal."

The candlelight caught the silver in his hair as Manny's smile deepened. "Then perhaps we should see what happens when the waters are calmer. After all," he added, lifting his glass in a toast, "we still have one more day. Perhaps you will allow me to show you Palma de Mallorca tomorrow?"

"To calmer waters," Tessa agreed, touching her glass to his, the crystal ringing with a clarity that seemed to promise something new beginning.

* * *

Tessa awoke to feel the gentle rocking of the ship and the warmth of Manny's arm draped across her. His presence provided an inexplicable comfort after the whirlwind of recent events. As he shifted beside her, she opened her eyes to see him sitting up, silhouetted against the dim light filtering through the curtains.

"Where are you going?" Her voice was a soft murmur in the still cabin.

Manny smiled down at her, a hint of apology in his gaze. "I've got to be on the bridge to guide us into port. It's Palma de Mallorca today."

She nodded, a sleepy yawn escaping despite herself. Manny brushed a stray hair from her cheek, his touch lingering. "Get some more sleep, Tessa. Meet me at eight-thirty, and we'll go ashore, sì?"

"Alright," she agreed, nestling back under the covers as Manny rose and dressed.

An hour later, Tessa shuffled back to her suite, the corridors still whispering with early-morning quiet. Her rumpled blue dress clung to her like a lingering memory of last night, and she carried her shoes, feet bare against the cool, smooth floor. Passing a few crew members, she caught knowing smiles and discreet nods, their expressions confirming what her tousled appearance subtly betrayed. A faint smile tugged at her lips as she replayed the night in her mind, her heart lighter, anticipation for the day ahead bubbling quietly inside her.

Chapter 18

The five friends gathered at the ship's café for a continental breakfast before exploring their final port of call. Sunlight streamed through the windows, illuminating the spread of croissants, fruit, and coffee as they claimed a table overlooking Palma de Mallorca's glittering harbor.

Tessa arrived last, and there was something undeniably different about her. Her silver bob caught the light differently, or perhaps it was the way she carried herself: shoulders relaxed, eyes bright with an inner glow that hadn't been there yesterday. She moved with a new lightness, as if some invisible weight had been lifted. When she smiled, it reached her eyes and lingered there, transforming her entire face.

"Someone's in a good mood this morning," Julia observed, exchanging knowing glances with Seren.

"I'd say more than good," Seren added, buttering a croissant with exaggerated focus. "I'd say our Tessa is positively radiant."

Kelly watched her mother over the rim of her coffee cup. "So… are you going to tell us what the captain had to say last night? About the arrests?"

"And anything else that might have happened after the official explanations?" Liam added with a mischievous grin.

Tessa took a delicate bite of her pastry, her eyes dancing with secrets she wasn't quite ready to share. "All in good time. I promise to tell you everything, but I'm meeting Manny in fifteen minutes. He's going to show me around Palma today."

Kelly studied her mother with genuine happiness. It had been years since she'd seen that sparkle in Tessa's eyes, perhaps not since before the troubles with her father began.

"What about the rest of you?" Tessa asked, deftly changing the subject. "Any plans for our last port day?"

Kelly set down her coffee cup. "Liam and I thought we'd hit the beach. Apparently, there's a gorgeous one just outside the city. Either of you interested?" she asked, looking at Julia and Seren.

"I've booked us a private tour of the island," Seren replied. "There's an olive press I'm dying to see, and Julia wants to visit the monastery at Valldemossa for inspiration."

As they finished breakfast, they made plans to meet for their traditional pre-dinner cocktails. Tessa checked her watch and stood, smoothing her sundress.

"Don't do anything I wouldn't do," Kelly called after her mother.

Tessa turned back with a smile that contained both innocence and mischief. "Darling, I think we've established that ship has already sailed."

* * *

Manny and Tessa walked down the pier, the Mediterranean breeze lifting Tessa's silver bob as they made their way toward the lineup of private tour guides and taxis. The morning sun cast long shadows across the harbor, where fishing boats bobbed alongside luxury yachts against a backdrop of Palma's honey-colored buildings.

177

"There he is." Manny pointed toward a driver in a crisp white shirt holding a sign that read "Captain Delgado." He said, "The Excursions Director called ahead for me. I told her we wanted something special today, away from the usual tourist routes."

The driver, a middle-aged Mallorcan with sun-weathered skin and kind eyes, greeted them with a warm smile. "Welcome to Palma, Captain. Señora." He gestured toward a glossy Mercedes parked nearby. "I am Rafeal. It will be my pleasure to show you our beautiful island today."

Once settled in the luxury car's cool interior, Manny leaned forward. "We'd like to avoid the crowds if possible. Something more… intimate."

"Of course, Captain. I know just the places." Rafeal nodded, understanding exactly what was being requested. "I will take you where the locals go, where you can experience the true Mallorca."

As they drove through Palma's narrow streets, the ancient city revealed itself, a blend of Gothic grandeur and Moorish influence. Rafeal navigated away from the bustling main thoroughfares, taking them through quiet squares where locals lingered over morning coffee.

Their first stop was the Arab Baths, nearly empty at this early hour. Walking through the peaceful garden with its softly burbling fountain, Tessa felt Manny's hand brush against hers before gently taking it.

"You mentioned Kelly is engaged?" Manny asked, his voice soft against the tranquil backdrop.

Tessa nodded, her face brightening. "Yes, to a wonderful woman named Briana. I've only spoken to her briefly on video calls, but Kelly is clearly so happy."

"And you? How do you feel about becoming a mother-in-law?"

"Honestly? I'm thrilled for her. Kelly kept her sexuality hidden from me for so long... I hate that she felt she couldn't tell me." Tessa paused, watching the play of light through the ancient stone arches. "What about you, Manny? Have you ever been married?"

Manny's eyes took on a distant look. "Once, many years ago. Elena traveled with me at first. She loved the romance of it, a captain's wife, sailing the world." His thumb traced small circles on Tessa's hand. "But after a year, the reality set in. The small cabin, the long separations when she stayed ashore, the constant movement... She moved back to Naples, and eventually, we divorced."

"I'm sorry."

"It was a long time ago. We were too young, perhaps." He shrugged philosophically. "This life, it's not for everyone. Most women cannot handle it, the isolation, the way time works differently at sea."

They wandered from the baths to Bellver Castle, climbing to its circular ramparts where the view stretched across the entire bay. Leaning against the ancient stone, Tessa felt a curious peace settle over her.

"I feel a bit rudderless since retiring," she admitted. "For decades, my identity was wrapped up in being a lawyer, a partner. Now suddenly there's all this... space. Empty time, I don't know how to fill."

"What would you fill it with if you could do anything?" Manny's eyes were curious, genuinely interested.

"Travel, I think. I've always wanted to see more of the world, but never had time beyond quick business trips." She laughed softly.

"And now that I have the time, I find myself sitting in Julia's condo watching Netflix instead."

"Perhaps you need a compass more than an anchor," Manny suggested, his eyes crinkling at the corners as he smiled.

By midday, they descended from the castle, and Rafeal drove them to a small restaurant perched on a cliff overlooking the sea. The terrace was nearly empty, a single table set apart from the others, dressed in white linen with a bottle of local wine already chilling.

"I took the liberty," Rafeal explained with a wink before discreetly disappearing.

Manny pulled out Tessa's chair, his hand lingering briefly on her shoulder.

* * *

As they settled into their cliffside table, the waiter poured them each a glass of golden Prensal Blanc wine. The view was spectacular, azure waters stretching to the horizon, the cathedral's spires visible in the distance, bathed in the gentle Mediterranean light.

"What comes next for you?" Tessa asked, swirling her wine. "Back to the Iridessa once she's out of dry dock?"

Manny leaned back, his silver hair catching the sunlight. "I have options." His fingers tapped lightly against the stem of his glass. "I could stay with the Aurelia for another month, return to the Iridessa after that, or take some shore leave until the Iridessa is ready."

"This afternoon," Manny continued, "I have a virtual meeting with nautical operations to discuss my plans. I will see what they have in mind."

"Who will take over?" Tessa began to ask just as the waiter arrived with their first course.

"Señor, señora… today we have prepared gambas al ajillo to start, followed by lubina a la sal." The waiter presented plump garlic prawns sizzling in earthenware, releasing an aroma of olive oil, chili, and garlic that made Tessa's mouth water.

For their main course, the waiter ceremoniously cracked open a salt crust to reveal perfectly cooked sea bass. He filleted it tableside, drizzling it with a simple sauce of olive oil, lemon, and fresh herbs.

"This reminds me of our dinner in Catania," Tessa said, savoring a bite of the delicate fish. "I've eaten so well on this trip, those pistachios we tried, the pasta in Rome, even that incredible bouillabaisse in Marseille."

"Food here tells our history," Manny replied, relaxing into safer conversation. "Arabs brought rice and spices, Greeks brought olives, Romans brought wine…"

"The Mediterranean diet," Tessa nodded. "I could get used to this way of eating. Fresh, simple, but so flavorful."

After lunch, they continued their tour, visiting the labyrinthine streets of Palma's Old Town. Walking through the dappled shade of narrow alleyways, Tessa caught Manny watching her several times, his expression thoughtful, as if weighing something in his mind.

"What are you thinking?" she finally asked as they paused in a quiet courtyard.

Manny smiled, but his eyes remained pensive. "Just enjoying the day."

Later, as they climbed the steps to Palma Cathedral, Tessa spoke of her plans, or lack thereof. "I should be looking for a house, but I can't decide where. Julia's moved to the Eastern Shore now that she's with Reid. Seren's barely in the country these days with all her retreat centers."

She ran her hand along the ancient stone wall. "I don't need to be near the office anymore. I could live anywhere, really, but that's the problem: too many choices, no clear direction."

Manny squeezed her hand gently. "It will work out. Sometimes the right path reveals itself when you're not looking so hard."

The afternoon slipped away too quickly. As the sun began its descent, casting long shadows across the city, Rafeal drove them back to the harbor. The Aurelia waited, glinting white against the darkening blue water.

At the gangway, Manny turned to Tessa. "Dinner with your friends tonight?"

She nodded. "I should catch up with them, see how their day was since I bailed out on them."

"After, perhaps… a nightcap in my quarters?" His question carried the weight of more than a simple invitation.

Tessa studied his face, trying to read what lay behind his careful expression. "I'll be there."

* * *

Moonlight spilled through the balcony doors of the captain's quarters, casting silver patterns across the rumpled sheets. Tessa lay with her head resting on Manny's chest, listening to his heartbeat gradually

182

slow to its normal rhythm. His fingers traced lazy patterns along her bare shoulder as they both basked in the comfortable silence that follows intimacy.

"Tell me about your friends," Manny murmured, his voice a pleasant rumble beneath her ear. "Did they enjoy Palma today?"

Tessa smiled, shifting slightly to look up at him. "They had a wonderful day. Julia and Seren took that island tour they'd booked. The monastery at Valldemossa apparently exceeded Julia's expectations; she filled three pages in her notebook with story ideas. And Seren found an ancient olive press that she's already scheming to turn into a retreat center."

"And Kelly? Did she enjoy the beach?"

"She and Liam had a perfect day, apparently. They found a little cove away from the crowds where they swam and read books. Kelly said the water was so clear she could see fish darting around her feet." Tessa chuckled softly. "She's already planning to bring Briana back here next summer."

Manny's hand stilled on her shoulder. "And did you tell them? About the investigation?"

"Everything," Tessa confirmed. "They were absolutely stunned when I explained about Vivian being an FBI agent. Seren kept interrupting, 'I knew there was something about that woman!' and Julia just sat there shaking her head in disbelief. Kelly was impressed with the whole operation, actually. She said it was like something out of a movie."

"What about your theory that I was involved?" Manny asked, a hint of teasing in his voice.

Tessa playfully swatted his chest. "I admitted I was wrong about that, thank you very much. They were all quite smug about it, too, especially Julia. She kept saying she knew you were one of the good guys."

They fell silent again, comfortable in each other's presence. The gentle rocking of the ship and the distant sound of waves created a cocoon of tranquility around them.

After a while, Manny spoke again, his voice more serious. "I've been distracted today."

Tessa propped herself up on one elbow to look at him properly. "I noticed. Is something wrong?"

"No, nothing's wrong." His eyes searched hers in the dim light. "It's just… I've been thinking about us, about this unexpected connection. When I first saw you boarding in Valletta, I never imagined we would end up here."

"Neither did I," Tessa admitted. "A romantic attachment was the furthest thing from my mind when I planned this cruise. I was focused on celebrating my retirement, spending time with Julia and Seren…"

"And instead, you found yourself in the middle of an international criminal investigation." Manny's smile was wry.

"And in your bed," Tessa added, her voice soft. "Both were quite the surprise."

Manny reached up to trace the line of her jaw with his fingertips. "What we found together was so pleasantly unexpected. And now I find myself hating to see it pass."

The truth of his words settled between them, a gentle weight of possibility and regret. In just two days, the cruise would end. Their passengers would disperse, returning to their lives across the globe.

"What are you saying, Manny?" Tessa asked, her heart quickening despite her attempt to remain calm.

"I'm saying that I don't want to say goodbye," he replied simply. "And I'm wondering if you feel the same way."

Chapter 19

Tessa awoke the next morning wrapped in Manny's arms, his sheets tangled around them both. Through the windows, the Mediterranean gleamed under early light, already blue and beckoning. She lay still, listening to his steady breathing, feeling the gentle rise and fall of his chest against her back. The thought settled heavily upon her; today was their last full day on the ship. Tomorrow would dissolve into the chaos of disembarkation, luggage carts, passport checks, a taxi to the airport, then the transatlantic flight back to Maryland's waiting winter.

The prospect of returning to Baltimore held no appeal. Her apartment, Julia's apartment, technically, would be cold and empty. The city streets would be gray and wet, nothing like the sun-soaked ports they'd visited these past eleven days.

Her thoughts spun in restless circles. What would fill her days now? Retirement stretched before her, formless and vast. She'd worked sixty-hour weeks for decades, driven by ambition and necessity. Now, with nothing demanding her attention, what would give her purpose? She could visit Kelly and Briana in San Francisco, but that would offer only a temporary diversion. Perhaps she could teach law at her alma mater? Take up yoga? Learn to paint? Nothing seemed to fit as she lay there contemplating the bleakness of Baltimore in January.

Beside her, Manny stirred, his arm tightening around her waist as he pressed his face into her hair.

"Buongiorno, bella," he murmured, his voice rough with sleep. "What time is it?"

Tessa glanced at the bedside clock. "Almost six."

He groaned softly. "I need to be on the bridge by seven." His lips found the curve of her neck. "Though I don't want to move from this spot."

"Can't you take the day off?" She turned in his arms to face him. "It's our last day."

Regret shadowed his eyes as he brushed a strand of silver hair from her face. "I wish I could. But I took yesterday off in Palma, and we have Barcelona tomorrow. The first officer has already covered more shifts than I should have asked."

Something sharp and sudden twisted in Tessa's chest, fear or resentment, she couldn't tell which. "I suppose you'll be too busy to see me today, then. And tomorrow I walk down the gangway, and you'll find some other passenger to charm the next week."

The words escaped before she could stop them. Manny's expression hardened, his eyes narrowing.

"Is that what you think?" He sat up, the sheets pooling around his waist. "That I make a habit of this? Taking women to my bed on every sailing?"

"Don't you?" The hurt in her voice surprised even her.

"No." His accent thickened with emotion. "I do not. In twenty-seven years at sea, I have never brought a passenger to my quarters." He ran a hand through his silver hair. "Do you not understand how different this is? How different you are to me?"

The fierceness in his voice made Tessa's anger dissolve. She sat up too, clutching the sheet to her chest.

"I'm sorry," she whispered. "That was unfair. I just…" She gestured helplessly. "I feel like we're breaking up before we've even begun. Like these past days have been some beautiful dream, and now I have to wake up and return to reality."

Manny's expression softened. He took her hands in his, thumbs stroking her knuckles.

"Listen to me, Tessa. I will not let that happen." His gaze held hers, unwavering. "We will work something out. This is not goodbye."

"But how?" The practical lawyer in her emerged. "You live on ships. It isn't as if I can meet you for dinner or spend the night at your apartment."

* * *

"We'll find a way," Manny insisted, though the path forward remained unclear to them both.

With reluctance, they finally pulled themselves from the warmth of the bed. Tessa gathered her clothes from where they'd been hastily discarded the night before, slipping into her dress as Manny watched her with undisguised appreciation.

"I should go before your staff arrives," she said, attempting to smooth her hair with her fingers. "I'm meeting everyone for breakfast at eight."

Manny crossed to her, still bare-chested, and drew her into his arms for one more lingering kiss. "I will see you later today. Somehow."

After Tessa slipped out, checking the corridor was empty before hurrying toward the elevator, Manny stood alone in his quarters. The faint scent of her perfume lingered in the air, a reminder of what he stood to lose in less than twenty-four hours.

He showered, letting the hot water cascade over his shoulders as he considered his options. Today's schedule was packed: routine safety inspections, systems checks, a meeting with his senior staff about tomorrow's turnover, and that virtual conference with the operations director about his next assignment. The day would pass quickly, with scarcely a moment to see Tessa.

Stepping out of the shower, he caught his reflection in the steamy mirror. The face looking back at him was that of a man torn between two loves.

Manny dressed methodically in his crisp white uniform, his movements automatic after decades of the same routine. He'd been honest with Tessa from the moment he met her on the Iridessa; something about her had captivated him. This week together had only deepened that initial attraction into something more substantial, more real than anything he'd felt in years.

There had been women in his life, of course. Brief shore romances, a failed marriage, and occasional companions during his leaves. But nothing like this—nothing that made him question the life he'd built.

As he made his coffee, Manny contemplated retirement. He was eligible, twenty-three years with the company next spring. He could take his pension, buy a villa somewhere on the coast, and perhaps consult occasionally. But even as he considered it, he knew he couldn't surrender the sea. The rhythmic pulse of engines beneath his feet, the endless horizon, the responsibility of guiding a floating city safely across the world's oceans; these things were woven into the fabric of his being.

A ship captain's life was one of constant motion and profound isolation. A captain never truly had any address, and the space they lived in was always occupied, never owned. Six months at sea, then a few weeks ashore. Holidays missed, birthdays celebrated via video call, relationships conducted largely through emails and brief phone conversations during port calls. His quarters, luxurious as they were, remained temporary, a space he occupied but never truly owned.

He'd watched colleagues try to balance this life with marriage and family. Some managed, most didn't. He'd often wished for a partner who understood this existence, who might even share it with him, but he'd long ago accepted that it was perhaps too much to ask.

Setting his empty coffee cup down with purpose, Manny straightened his jacket and secured his captain's hat. As he headed for the bridge, determination settled in his chest. There had to be a solution; he just hadn't found it yet. The operations meeting later might provide an opening.

* * *

The deck sparkled under Mediterranean sunshine, a perfect final day at sea. Julia arrived early, securing a prime table beneath a white canvas awning where the breeze carried just a hint of salt. When Tessa appeared minutes later, Julia immediately recognized the clouds behind her friend's smile.

"You've already had coffee," Julia observed as Tessa slid into her seat. "And not enough sleep."

Tessa managed a weak laugh. "That obvious?"

"Only to someone who's known you for forty years." Julia reached across the table, covering Tessa's fidgeting hands with her own. "What's wrong? Did something happen to Manny?"

Tessa glanced around to ensure their privacy before leaning forward. "I'm a mess, Jules. Actual tears this morning, like some lovesick teenager."

"You've fallen for him."

"Completely." Tessa sighed, her shoulders dropping. "I had no intention of getting involved with anyone on this cruise, with any man, period. My life was supposed to be about finding myself post-divorce, post-career. And now here I am, heartbroken before we've even said goodbye."

A server appeared with fresh orange juice and pastries. They both smiled automatically, waiting until he departed before continuing.

"You know," Julia said, selecting a croissant, "there are ways to make this work if you both want it badly enough."

"Such as?"

"You could fly out to meet him in different ports. Book another cruise on his ship once you know his schedule." Julia broke the pastry in half, releasing a cloud of buttery steam.

"I don't know. Manny's constantly moving; different ports, different ships. And do I really want to be the woman who chases a man around the globe?" Tessa's voice lowered. "I sound pathetic."

"You sound like someone who found something unexpected and precious." Julia's eyes softened. "Besides, who says you'd be chasing him? You're retired now. The whole world is open to you."

Tessa stirred her coffee absently. "How do you do it, Jules? Fill your days now that you're not working eighty hours a week?"

Julia considered this. "Some days I'm bored, I won't lie. Writing helps, gives me structure. And things with Reid are still new enough that we're discovering each other. But there are still mornings when I wake up and think, 'What am I supposed to do today?'"

"That's what I'm afraid of," Tessa admitted. "Going home to an empty condo with nothing but time stretching out in front of me."

The conversation paused as Seren approached their table, wrapped in a flowing turquoise caftan that billowed behind her like a sail.

"Well, don't you two look serious on such a gorgeous morning." Seren dropped into an empty chair, immediately sensing the mood. Her smile faded as she studied Tessa's face. "Oh, honey. You're thinking about tomorrow already, aren't you?"

Tessa nodded, grateful for Seren's perceptiveness.

"She's fallen hard for our dashing captain," Julia explained.

"Of course she has. We all saw that coming a mile away." Seren reached over to squeeze Tessa's wrist. "The question is what you're going to do about it."

"That's what we were discussing," Julia said. "The logistics of dating a man who lives on ships."

Seren waved a hand dismissively. "Logistics are just details, darling. If it matters enough, you find a way."

"Says the woman who's managed three marriages," Tessa retorted, but with affection.

"And I regret none of them." Seren's eyes sparkled. "Life's too short not to follow your heart when it speaks to you. Especially at our age."

A server refilled their coffee cups as they fell into contemplative silence. The ship glided smoothly through calm blue waters, leaving a frothy white wake that dissolved into the vastness of the Mediterranean.

"When I was twenty-five," Seren began, "I fell madly in love with a man who traveled constantly for work. Oil rigs, remote construction sites, he was gone for months at a time. My mother told me I was insane to even consider it." She smiled at the memory. "We had seven wonderful years together before he died. Not once did I regret choosing love over convenience."

"Was that Gerald?" Julia asked.

"No, darling. Before Gerald. He was the reason I learned to travel light and adapt quickly." Seren leaned toward Tessa. "The point is, sometimes the heart knows what it wants before the head has figured out the details."

Tessa's response was cut short as she spotted Kelly approaching their table, her face bright in the morning sun.

"Morning, everyone," Kelly called, pulling out a chair. "What are we discussing so intensely? Last-day activities? Packing strategies?"

"Just enjoying our final breakfast at sea," Tessa replied, smoothly changing the subject. "How did you sleep?"

As Kelly launched into a story about her late-night conference call, Tessa tried hard to focus, with little success.

Chapter 20

As breakfast wound down, the four friends began to disperse across the ship for their final day at sea. The thought of saying goodbye lingered beneath the buzz of last-day plans, giving the table a bittersweet atmosphere.

"I need to find Liam," Kelly announced, checking her phone. "He has some connections in the venture capital world. I want to pick his brain about it before we dock tomorrow."

Julia gathered her notebook and reading glasses." And I'm off to the Port Talk about Barcelona. They're covering some hidden gems beyond the usual tourist spots." She squeezed Tessa's shoulder. "Think about what we discussed, okay?"

As the others drifted away, Seren lingered, studying Tessa's face with the intuitive perception that had made her such a successful businesswoman. "You're still brooding, darling. Come with me to my suite. I could use your legal expertise on something, and it might take your mind off tomorrow."

Tessa welcomed the distraction. "Lead the way."

In Seren's suite, floor-to-ceiling windows showcased the endless blue horizon as Seren retrieved a leather portfolio from her carry-on. "The buyers for Marwood Travels sent over their final contract yesterday. The purchase price is excellent, but the non-compete clause is giving me pause."

She handed Tessa several pages of legal text. Tessa slipped on her reading glasses and began scanning the document with practiced efficiency.

"Seller agrees not to engage, directly or indirectly, in any business that competes with or is substantially similar to Marwood Travels within the global marketplace for a period of ten years," Tessa read aloud, her attorney's mind immediately identifying the issues. "This includes but is not limited to: booking travel accommodations, arranging transportation, organizing tours, providing travel consultation services, or marketing travel-related products or services."

She continued reading silently, her frown deepening. "This is incredibly broad, Seren. Under these terms, you couldn't even blog about your personal travel experiences if your posts contained recommendations."

"Exactly my concern," Seren replied, settling into a chair across from Tessa. "I'm happy to step away from Marwood Travels as a full-service agency, but my retreat business often involves arranging travel packages for participants. I can't have my hands completely tied."

Tessa grabbed a pen from the desk and began making notes in the margins. "We need to narrow the scope geographically, reduce the time period, and carve out specific exceptions for your retreat business."

For the next thirty minutes, Tessa crafted alternative language, her legal mind fully engaged for the first time since retirement. She proposed limiting the non-compete to specific regions where Marwood Travels had established clientele, reducing the term to five years, and explicitly exempting travel arrangements connected to wellness retreats.

"Here," she said finally, sliding the marked-up document across to Seren. "This gives them reasonable protection for their investment while preserving your ability to operate your retreat business without constant worry about breaching the agreement."

Seren reviewed Tessa's suggestions, nodding appreciatively. "This is brilliant, Tess. Exactly what I needed."

"Have you considered retaining a minority stake instead of selling outright?" Tessa asked. "It might give you more flexibility moving forward, plus continued income."

Seren's eyes sparkled with that familiar gleam that appeared whenever she was plotting something. "I've considered it, but I need the full capital for an investment opportunity I've had my eye on."

"What kind of investment?" Tessa's curiosity was piqued.

"Not quite ready to share those details," Seren replied with a mysterious smile. "Let's just say it involves beautiful Mediterranean views and ancient olive trees."

Tessa raised an eyebrow. "Sounds intriguing."

"It will be." Seren gathered the papers, her expression turning thoughtful. "You know, Tess, you're absolutely brilliant at this. Have you considered offering your services to small businesses on a volunteer basis? So many entrepreneurs can't afford someone with your expertise, but they desperately need it."

"I hadn't thought about it," Tessa admitted, surprised by how satisfying the past half hour had been.

"The Maryland Women's Business Center would snatch you up in a heartbeat. You could set your own hours, choose projects that interest you, make a real difference without the pressure of billable hours and demanding clients."

Tessa found herself genuinely considering the idea. "It would give me some structure without the stress of practicing full-time."

"And purpose," Seren added gently. "Which we all need, regardless of our age or relationship status."

Tessa caught the subtext in Seren's words that finding fulfillment in her professional life didn't preclude pursuing whatever was developing with Manny. Perhaps they could complement each other.

"I'll think about it," she promised, feeling a subtle shift in her perspective. For the first time since retiring, she glimpsed a future that wasn't defined by what she was leaving behind, but by what might lie ahead.

"That's all I ask," Seren said, squeezing her hand. "Now, shall we enjoy our last afternoon at sea?"

* * *

The afternoon sun glinted off the polished railings of the Aurelia's aft deck as Liam McDougal paced the promenade, his normally composed demeanor replaced with agitated energy. His phone pressed tightly against his ear, he gestured emphatically with his free hand, unaware of being observed.

Through a window from the indoor lounge, Kelly spotted him. She'd been looking for Liam to get his opinion on a potential acquisition her firm was considering, a promising AI healthcare startup that seemed perfect for their portfolio. She pushed open the heavy glass door to the deck, the warm Mediterranean breeze greeting her as she stepped outside.

"No, Daniel, that's not how this works," Liam's voice carried across the otherwise empty deck. "You can't sell the condo without my agreement. Every piece of antique furniture in there is mine, and you have absolutely no right to liquidate any of it."

Kelly slowed her approach, realizing she'd walked into a private moment. She considered retreating, but Liam had already seen her.

"The condo will sell faster and easier if left as is," Liam continued, his voice rising with frustration. "For God's sake, I paid a substantial sum to have Nate Berkus do the design. The place is practically a showcase."

Kelly began to turn away, not wanting to eavesdrop on what was clearly the messy aftermath of a relationship breakdown, but Liam held up his hand, signaling her to wait.

"Honestly, I don't even care about the condo," Liam said, his tone hardening. "I never liked living in New York. I moved there for you, for your career. Remember?" He paused, listening. "Well, that's revisionist history if I ever heard it."

Liam's jaw tightened as he listened to whatever Daniel was saying on the other end of the line. The veins in his neck stood out prominently.

"This conversation is going nowhere," he finally said. "My attorney will be sending documents over for you to sign tomorrow. As soon as I return to New York, I'll place the condo up for sale and have my belongings removed." With that, he jabbed the end call button with such force, it seemed he might crack his screen.

Liam took a deep breath, composed himself, and turned to Kelly with an apologetic smile. "Sorry you had to witness that undignified display. Not my finest moment."

"No apology necessary," Kelly replied, attempting to lighten the mood. "Though I have to ask, did you really have Nate Berkus design your condo?"

Liam's tension visibly eased. "I did, actually. It was the one extravagance I insisted upon. Daniel thought it was ridiculous, but I wanted something that felt like… home." His voice softened on the last word.

"Well, now you're going to need somewhere new to call home," Kelly observed, leaning against the railing beside him.

"Yes, I suppose I am." Liam looked out at the endless blue horizon, seeming suddenly untethered.

Kelly studied him thoughtfully. "I've been doing some discreet research, you know. Testing you a little over these past ten days."

Liam turned to her, eyebrow raised. "Have you now?"

"My team discovered that Vaughn Capital hasn't been performing particularly well, despite you bringing in several high-profile clients."

"Your intelligence is accurate," Liam admitted, not seeming surprised by her knowledge. "The firm's senior partners are… let's just say their investment philosophy is increasingly at odds with current market realities."

Kelly nodded, having suspected as much. "Vertex Ventures is planning to expand our New York operations, but we also need to strengthen our San Francisco headquarters." She paused, gauging his reaction. "I could use someone with your skills and connections, Liam."

Liam's expression shifted from surprise to intrigue. "Are you offering me a job?"

"I am. You could stay in New York if you prefer, but I'd rather have you in San Francisco." Kelly's tone was professional, but her eyes conveyed something more personal. "I've enjoyed your friendship these past days. I'd like to have you nearby."

Liam stared at her, momentarily speechless. "Kelly, that's… I don't know what to say. It's an incredibly generous offer."

"You don't have to answer now," she assured him. "Take some time to think about it. We're both heading back to our real lives tomorrow. But know the offer is genuine."

Liam nodded slowly, his gaze returning to the sea. "Thank you. I will definitely give it serious consideration."

The two stood in companionable silence, watching the wake of the ship stretch out behind them—a temporary mark on the vast ocean that would soon vanish, just as their time aboard the Aurelia was coming to an end. But perhaps, Kelly thought, it was also the beginning of something new.

* * *

Captain Delgado straightened his uniform jacket as he entered the meeting room, the space empty save for the large monitor on the wall and the conference table with its polished surface reflecting the Mediterranean sunlight streaming through the windows. He placed his tablet and a notepad precisely in front of the center chair, then checked his watch, two minutes early, as always.

At exactly 1400 hours, he initiated the connection. The Selene Voyages logo appeared briefly on screen before transitioning to the video feed from corporate headquarters. Manny was surprised to find only Eduardo Vega, the Director of Fleet Operations, staring back at him rather than the usual array of captains and executives.

"Good afternoon, Captain Delgado," Eduardo greeted him. "I hope I find you well?"

"Very well, thank you," Manny replied, slightly puzzled by the private call. "Is there a problem with the others joining?"

Eduardo shook his head. "No problem at all. I wanted a few minutes with you privately before bringing in the rest of the team." He leaned forward, his expression warm. "First, let me congratulate you again on the successful Interpol operation. The way you and your team handled the situation was exemplary: discreet, professional, and with minimal disruption to the guests' experience."

"Thank you, sir. Has there been any reaction from the other passengers?"

"That's what's remarkable, not a single complaint or inquiry has reached us," Eduardo replied. "As far as we can tell, only those directly involved had any idea what was happening. A testament to your discretion."

Manny nodded, relieved. "Has there been news coverage?"

"Some, yes. Our PR department is managing it beautifully." Eduardo smiled. "You're being portrayed as something of a hero, Manny. 'Veteran captain assists international authorities in dismantling luxury cruise crime ring.' The company couldn't buy that kind of positive publicity."

"I was simply doing my job," Manny demurred.

"And doing it exceptionally well, which brings me to the real purpose of this private conversation." Eduardo straightened in his chair, his expression turning more formal. "The company has a proposition for you, Captain Delgado."

Manny felt a flutter of anticipation. "I'm listening."

"We would like to offer you command of the *Celestia,* our newest vessel."

Manny's eyebrows rose. The *Celestia* had been the talk of the industry for months, a state-of-the-art ship designed specifically for extended voyages, with technological innovations and luxury amenities unlike anything in their current fleet.

"The *Celestia* will embark on her maiden voyage in two weeks," Eduardo continued. "A full world cruise:180 days visiting 87 ports across 32 countries." He leaned closer to the camera. "The itinerary includes several overnight stays in select destinations and longer port calls overall. We want our guests to have a more immersive experience than traditional cruises offer."

Manny's mind raced. Command of a new vessel was the highest honor in the company, usually reserved for captains with seniority and spotless records. The *Celestia* would be the crown jewel of the fleet.

"What about Captain Spencer? I thought he was assigned to the Celestia." Manny asked.

"He was," Eduardo agreed. "Unfortunately, he has become ill and cannot accept the assignment. So, we want you."

"This is… quite an honor," Manny said carefully. "May I ask how long I have to consider the offer?"

Eduardo laughed. "About two minutes, I'm afraid. I'd like to announce your assignment when I bring the rest of the team into this call."

Manny's thoughts immediately turned to Tessa. A world cruise, she would love that. The immersive port experiences, the diversity of cultures, and the leisurely pace of discovery. It was everything she'd mentioned wanting in her retirement. But would she come with him? The idea of spending six months exploring the world with Tessa by his side made his heart race.

If she joined him, the *Celestia* would become more than just a ship under his command; it would be a home they shared, a place where they could build something together without either having to give up what mattered to them. She could have her global adventures, and he could have the sea he loved… and they could have each other.

It was a perfect solution to the problem that had been gnawing at him since last night. But it required a leap of faith, a belief that what they'd found in these eleven days was substantial enough for Tessa to rearrange her entire life.

"Captain?" Eduardo prompted. "I don't mean to rush you, but the others are waiting to join."

Manny took a deep breath. He thought of Tessa's eyes lighting up when she spoke of travel, of how quickly she'd adapted to life at sea, of the way she'd fit so naturally into his world. It was a gamble, but some instinct told him it was the right one.

"I accept the assignment," he said firmly. "It would be my honor to captain the *Celestia* on her maiden voyage."

Eduardo's face broke into a broad smile. "Excellent! I was hoping you'd say that. Now, let's bring in the others and make it official."

Chapter 21

The Mediterranean sun cast diamond-like sparkles across the pool's surface as Tessa, Julia, and Seren lounged on adjacent deck chairs. Their final day at sea had taken on a bittersweet quality, each moment precious precisely because it was fleeting.

"I don't think I'll ever tire of this view," Julia murmured, her notebook open but forgotten on her lap as she gazed at the endless horizon.

Seren adjusted her wide-brimmed hat against the breeze. "The sky meets the sea so perfectly it's almost unnatural. Like someone painted it."

Tessa nodded absently, her thoughts adrift. Since her conversation with Manny that morning, a restlessness had settled into her bones. Each hour that passed was one less they had together, yet he was consumed with duties she couldn't interrupt.

"You're doing it again," Seren observed, peering at Tessa over her sunglasses.

"Doing what?"

"That thing with your fingers. Tapping like you're waiting for something." Seren reached over to still Tessa's hand. "He'll find time for you today. That man is besotted."

Before Tessa could respond, a white-uniformed crew member appeared beside her chair, a silver tray in his hands. On it sat a folded note with the captain's insignia embossed in gold.

"Ms. Monroe," the young man said formally. "Captain Delgado asked me to deliver this to you personally."

All three women straightened, their attention instantly riveted to the note. Tessa accepted it with fingers that trembled slightly despite her attempt to appear casual.

"Thank you," she managed, waiting until the crew member departed before unfolding the paper.

Tessa,

I must see you immediately. Please come to my quarters as soon as you receive this. It's urgent.

Yours,

Manny

The brevity and formality of the message sent a chill through her despite the warm sun. No explanation, no hint of what awaited her… just urgency.

"What is it?" Julia asked, leaning forward.

Tessa passed her the note. "He wants to see me right away."

"That sounds serious," Seren said, reading over Julia's shoulder.

"And a bit mysterious," Julia added. "He doesn't say why."

"I hope nothing's wrong." Tessa stood quickly, gathering her belongings. Her mind raced through possibilities… had something happened with the investigation? Was there some problem with their disembarkation tomorrow? Or was it something more personal?

"Go," Seren urged, helping Tessa collect her sunscreen and book. "We'll be right here when you get back."

Tessa slipped on her white linen cover-up, suddenly conscious of her appearance. Her hair was wind-tousled, her face bare of makeup. "I should change first."

"Absolutely not," Julia insisted. "He said immediately. Besides," her eyes twinkled "… he's seen you in far less than a swimsuit and cover-up."

Tessa felt heat rise to her cheeks as Seren laughed in agreement.

"I promise to tell you everything as soon as I can," she said, slinging her bag over her shoulder. "Whatever 'urgent' means."

She walked quickly through the ship, heart pounding with a mixture of anticipation and anxiety. Crew members nodded respectfully as she passed by now, most recognized her as the captain's special guest. The familiarity both pleased and pained her; tomorrow, she would be just another departed passenger.

At the captain's quarters, a steward was waiting outside. He opened the door for her with a slight bow.

"The captain will join you shortly, ma'am. He asked that you make yourself comfortable."

The door closed behind her, leaving Tessa alone in the elegant sitting room. Afternoon light streamed through the windows, illuminating the polished wood and nautical art pieces she'd come to appreciate over the past few days. It felt both familiar and foreign, like a dream space that existed between reality and imagination.

She paced the room, too wound up to sit. What could be so urgent? The note hadn't sounded romantic, more businesslike and formal. Perhaps he'd decided a clean break was better. Perhaps he'd realized the impossibility of their situation and wanted to end things properly before Barcelona.

The click of the door interrupted her spiraling thoughts. Manny entered, still in his formal white uniform, his captain's hat tucked under his arm. His face was flushed, eyes bright with some barely contained emotion. He looked simultaneously exhausted and exhilarated.

"Tessa," he breathed, as though her name itself brought him relief. "Thank you for coming so quickly."

"Your note sounded urgent. Is everything alright?"

"Sí, sí, better than alright." He set his hat on the desk, gesturing toward the sofa. "Please, sit. I have something important to tell you."

The nervous energy coming off him was palpable. Tessa sat, perched on the edge of the cushion as Manny settled beside her, angling his body to face hers. He took both her hands in his, his expression earnest.

"First, I want you to know how important you have become to me," he began, his accent thickening with emotion. "These days together… they have changed something in me. I find myself thinking of you constantly, even when I should be focused on the ship."

Tessa squeezed his hands, her heart racing. "I feel the same way."

"This morning, after you left, I was troubled about our future, how we could continue what we've found. The distance, the logistics…" He paused, gathering his thoughts. "Then, just hours ago, I was offered an extraordinary opportunity. A new assignment."

Tessa nodded, showing she was listening, though uncertainty flickered through her.

"I have been named captain of the *Celestia*, our newest ship, the most advanced in our fleet. She embarks on her maiden voyage in two weeks." His eyes shone with pride. "A world cruise, Tessa. One hundred and eighty-seven days at sea, visiting thirty-two countries across six continents. The itinerary includes extended stays in many ports, two, three days in some places, allowing for real exploration, not just brief glimpses."

Understanding dawned on her. "You took a new assignment today? Without knowing if..."

"It was a leap of faith," he admitted. "I thought of you immediately, of how you spoke of wanting to travel, to see the world now that you're retired. I thought perhaps... perhaps we could do this together."

Tessa's mind reeled, trying to process what he was suggesting. "Together? You mean..."

"You must understand what it means to be the wife of a ship's captain," he continued earnestly. "It is not an easy life. You would share my quarters, which are comfortable but not a true home. There would be official functions where you would be expected to appear at my side. Guests would see you as an extension of the cruise line, someone they could approach with questions or concerns."

"Your wife?" Tessa interrupted, the word hanging between them. "Manny, are you... Are you asking me to marry you?"

He blinked, then nodded firmly. "Sí. We would have to marry if you were to accompany me on the cruise. The company's policy is clear: No unmarried partners living aboard, especially not in the captain's quarters. And I want you with me, Tessa. Not visiting occasionally or meeting in ports but sharing this life."

Stunned silence filled the room. Tessa stared at him, unable to form words. Marriage? After eleven days together? It seemed impossible, irrational, the kind of impulsive decision she'd spent a lifetime warning clients against.

Manny rushed to fill the silence, his words tumbling over each other. "Think of the places we would see together, the ancient temples of Angkor Wat at sunrise, cherry blossoms in Japan, the pristine beaches of Polynesia. We would sail the Suez Canal, drop anchor in Antarctica's icy waters, cross the equator beneath stars you've never seen." His hands tightened around hers. "And we would do it all together, Tessa. No goodbyes, no separation."

He paused, searching her face. "I know this is sudden. Unexpected. Perhaps even crazy. But when I accepted the assignment, I could only think of how perfect it would be to share it with you." His voice softened. "What are your thoughts?"

* * *

"Yes!"

The word burst from her lips before her rational mind could intervene. A single syllable swept away a lifetime of careful deliberation and measured decisions.

"Yes," she repeated, softer this time, as if trying the word on for size. Her eyes widened at her own spontaneity. "Oh my God. Did I just? I did. I said yes."

Manny's face transformed with relief and joy. He pulled her into his arms, burying his face in her hair. "Grazie a Dio," he murmured. "I thought perhaps I had lost my mind."

She pulled back suddenly, her mind racing to catch up with her heart. "But how? When? Where would we even? There's so much to arrange. I don't have a dress. We need witnesses. What about a license?"

"Today," Manny said firmly, taking her trembling hands in his. "It must be today, while we're still in international waters. After tomorrow, the legal complications become… significant."

Tessa's pulse quickened. "Today? As in… hours from now?"

"Six o'clock. In the ship's chapel." His smile was reassuring, excited. "The Staff Captain has just been promoted to full captain of the Aurelia as of this afternoon. He has the authority to perform marriages at sea."

"Six o'clock," Tessa echoed, glancing at her watch. Less than four hours. Her fingers flew to her hair, still damp from the pool. "But I need to tell Kelly! And Julia and Seren. Oh God, what will I wear? My luggage is already packed for disembarkation. I need to contact my lawyer about the power of attorney and…"

She began pacing, fingers tapping rapidly against her thigh as mental checklists formed and multiplied. "I'll need to sublease Julia's condo. Cancel my dentist appointment next week. What about my mail? And the retirement dinner the partners scheduled for next month."

Manny stepped into her path, gently placing his hands on her shoulders. "Tessa. Breathe." His voice was steady, a counterpoint to her frenetic energy. "I will handle everything for the ceremony. The flowers, the music, even a photographer. The cruise director owes me a favor; she can find something suitable for you to wear."

"But my daughter, I have to…"

"Yes, of course. Go, tell Kelly and your friends. They should be the first to know." He guided her toward the door, his hand warm against the small of her back. "I'll send someone to find them if you can't. But everything else? Leave it to me."

Tessa nodded, but her fingers were already twisting her necklace, her foot tapping against the carpet. "Rings. We need rings. And I should call my financial advisor. And"

"We sail with a jeweler aboard," Manny reminded her, amusement warming his voice. "One more thing to cross off your list."

He opened the door but held her there a moment longer, cupping her face in his hands. His expression shifted, becoming serious, almost reverent.

"Tessa," he said, his voice dropping to a near whisper. "I need you to know something before you go."

Her racing thoughts paused as she met his gaze.

"I love you." The words emerged unambiguous. "It feels impossible after so short a time, but I know it as surely as I know the stars or the tides. I have lived a solitary life, married to the sea, until now. But I want to share whatever years I have left with you, at sea, on land, wherever we find ourselves."

Tears sprang to Tessa's eyes, unexpected and overwhelming. All her frantic energy dissolved into something deeper, more certain.

"I love you too," she whispered back, the truth of it resonating through her. "God help me, I do."

He kissed her then, gently, sweetly, before pulling away. "Six o'clock," he reminded her. "Don't be late."

"I won't," she promised, and with one last look at his beloved face, she hurried down the corridor.

As she rushed toward the pool where she'd left Julia and Seren, her mind raced with logistics and doubts and impossible excitement. Sixty-two years of careful planning, and now she was getting married to a ship captain she'd known for eleven days, in less than four hours.

It was madness. Complete, utter madness.

And yet, beneath the panic and practical concerns, a surprising sense of rightness had settled in her chest. For the first time in decades, perhaps in her entire life, she was following her heart instead of her head. Jumping without knowing exactly where she would land.

The realization made her laugh out loud as she rushed through the ship, drawing curious glances from passing guests. Tessa Monroe, cautious, pragmatic, always-prepared Tessa, was leaping into the unknown.

And it felt glorious.

Chapter 21

The Mediterranean sun cast diamond-like sparkles across the pool's surface as Tessa, Julia, and Seren lounged on adjacent deck chairs. Their final day at sea had taken on a bittersweet quality, each moment precious precisely because it was fleeting.

"I don't think I'll ever tire of this view," Julia murmured, her notebook open but forgotten on her lap as she gazed at the endless horizon.

Seren adjusted her wide-brimmed hat against the breeze. "The sky meets the sea so perfectly it's almost unnatural. Like someone painted it."

Tessa nodded absently, her thoughts adrift. Since her conversation with Manny that morning, a restlessness had settled into her bones. Each hour that passed was one less they had together, yet he was consumed with duties she couldn't interrupt.

"You're doing it again," Seren observed, peering at Tessa over her sunglasses.

"Doing what?"

"That thing with your fingers. Tapping like you're waiting for something." Seren reached over to still Tessa's hand. "He'll find time for you today. That man is besotted."

Before Tessa could respond, a white-uniformed crew member appeared beside her chair, a silver tray in his hands. On it sat a folded note with the captain's insignia embossed in gold.

"Ms. Monroe," the young man said formally. "Captain Delgado asked me to deliver this to you personally."

All three women straightened, their attention instantly riveted to the note. Tessa accepted it with fingers that trembled slightly despite her attempt to appear casual.

"Thank you," she managed, waiting until the crew member departed before unfolding the paper.

Tessa,

I must see you immediately. Please come to my quarters as soon as you receive this. It's urgent.

Yours,

Manny

The brevity and formality of the message sent a chill through her despite the warm sun. No explanation, no hint of what awaited her… just urgency.

"What is it?" Julia asked, leaning forward.

Tessa passed her the note. "He wants to see me right away."

"That sounds serious," Seren said, reading over Julia's shoulder.

"And a bit mysterious," Julia added. "He doesn't say why."

"I hope nothing's wrong." Tessa stood quickly, gathering her belongings. Her mind raced through possibilities… had something happened with the investigation? Was there some problem with their disembarkation tomorrow? Or was it something more personal?

"Go," Seren urged, helping Tessa collect her sunscreen and book. "We'll be right here when you get back."

Tessa slipped on her white linen cover-up, suddenly conscious of her appearance. Her hair was wind-tousled, her face bare of makeup. "I should change first."

"Absolutely not," Julia insisted. "He said immediately. Besides," her eyes twinkled "… he's seen you in far less than a swimsuit and cover-up."

Tessa felt heat rise to her cheeks as Seren laughed in agreement.

"I promise to tell you everything as soon as I can," she said, slinging her bag over her shoulder. "Whatever 'urgent' means."

She walked quickly through the ship, heart pounding with a mixture of anticipation and anxiety. Crew members nodded respectfully as she passed by now, most recognized her as the captain's special guest. The familiarity both pleased and pained her; tomorrow, she would be just another departed passenger.

At the captain's quarters, a steward was waiting outside. He opened the door for her with a slight bow.

"The captain will join you shortly, ma'am. He asked that you make yourself comfortable."

The door closed behind her, leaving Tessa alone in the elegant sitting room. Afternoon light streamed through the windows, illuminating the polished wood and nautical art pieces she'd come to appreciate over the past few days. It felt both familiar and foreign, like a dream space that existed between reality and imagination.

She paced the room, too wound up to sit. What could be so urgent? The note hadn't sounded romantic, more businesslike and formal. Perhaps he'd decided a clean break was better. Perhaps he'd realized the impossibility of their situation and wanted to end things properly before Barcelona.

The click of the door interrupted her spiraling thoughts. Manny entered, still in his formal white uniform, his captain's hat tucked under his arm. His face was flushed, eyes bright with some barely contained emotion. He looked simultaneously exhausted and exhilarated.

"Tessa," he breathed, as though her name itself brought him relief. "Thank you for coming so quickly."

"Your note sounded urgent. Is everything alright?"

" Sí, sí, better than alright." He set his hat on the desk, gesturing toward the sofa. "Please, sit. I have something important to tell you."

The nervous energy coming off him was palpable. Tessa sat, perched on the edge of the cushion as Manny settled beside her, angling his body to face hers. He took both her hands in his, his expression earnest.

"First, I want you to know how important you have become to me," he began, his accent thickening with emotion. "These days together… they have changed something in me. I find myself thinking of you constantly, even when I should be focused on the ship."

Tessa squeezed his hands, her heart racing. "I feel the same way."

"This morning, after you left, I was troubled about our future, how we could continue what we've found. The distance, the logistics…" He paused, gathering his thoughts. "Then, just hours ago, I was offered an extraordinary opportunity. A new assignment."

Tessa nodded, showing she was listening, though uncertainty flickered through her.

"I have been named captain of the *Celestia*, our newest ship, the most advanced in our fleet. She embarks on her maiden voyage in two weeks." His eyes shone with pride. "A world cruise, Tessa. One hundred and eighty-seven days at sea, visiting thirty-two countries across six continents. The itinerary includes extended stays in many ports, two, three days in some places, allowing for real exploration, not just brief glimpses."

Understanding dawned on her. "You took a new assignment today? Without knowing if"

"It was a leap of faith," he admitted. "I thought of you immediately, of how you spoke of wanting to travel, to see the world now that you're retired. I thought perhaps… perhaps we could do this together."

Tessa's mind reeled, trying to process what he was suggesting. "Together? You mean"

"You must understand what it means to be the wife of a ship's captain," he continued earnestly. "It is not an easy life. You would share my quarters, which are comfortable but not a true home. There would be official functions where you would be expected to appear at my side. Guests would see you as an extension of the cruise line, someone they could approach with questions or concerns."

"Your wife?" Tessa interrupted, the word hanging between them. "Manny, are you… Are you asking me to marry you?"

He blinked, then nodded firmly. "Sí. We would have to marry if you were to accompany me on the cruise. The company's policy is clear: No unmarried partners living aboard, especially not in the captain's quarters. And I want you with me, Tessa. Not visiting occasionally or meeting in ports but sharing this life."

Stunned silence filled the room. Tessa stared at him, unable to form words. Marriage? After eleven days together? It seemed impossible, irrational, the kind of impulsive decision she'd spent a lifetime warning clients against.

Manny rushed to fill the silence, his words tumbling over each other. "Think of the places we would see together, the ancient temples of Angkor Wat at sunrise, cherry blossoms in Japan, the pristine beaches of Polynesia. We would sail the Suez Canal, drop anchor in Antarctica's icy waters, cross the equator beneath stars you've never seen." His hands tightened around hers. "And we would do it all together, Tessa. No goodbyes, no separation."

He paused, searching her face. "I know this is sudden. Unexpected. Perhaps even crazy. But when I accepted the assignment, I could only think of how perfect it would be to share it with you." His voice softened. "What are your thoughts?"

* * *

"Yes!"

The word burst from her lips before her rational mind could intervene. A single syllable swept away a lifetime of careful deliberation and measured decisions.

"Yes," she repeated, softer this time, as if trying the word on for size. Her eyes widened at her own spontaneity. "Oh my God. Did I just? I did. I said yes."

Manny's face transformed with relief and joy. He pulled her into his arms, burying his face in her hair. "Grazie a Dio," he murmured. "I thought perhaps I had lost my mind."

She pulled back suddenly, her mind racing to catch up with her heart. "But how? When? Where would we even? There's so much to arrange. I don't have a dress. We need witnesses. What about a license?"

"Today," Manny said firmly, taking her trembling hands in his. "It must be today, while we're still in international waters. After tomorrow, the legal complications become… significant."

Tessa's pulse quickened. "Today? As in… hours from now?"

"Six o'clock. In the ship's chapel." His smile was reassuring, excited. "The Staff Captain has just been promoted to full captain of the Aurelia as of this afternoon. He has the authority to perform marriages at sea."

"Six o'clock," Tessa echoed, glancing at her watch. Less than four hours. Her fingers flew to her hair, still damp from the pool. "But I need to tell Kelly! And Julia and Seren. Oh God, what will I wear? My luggage is already packed for disembarkation. I need to contact my lawyer about the power of attorney and…"

She began pacing, fingers tapping rapidly against her thigh as mental checklists formed and multiplied. "I'll need to sublease Julia's condo. Cancel my dentist appointment next week. What about my mail? And the retirement dinner the partners scheduled for next month."

Manny stepped into her path, gently placing his hands on her shoulders. "Tessa. Breathe." His voice was steady, a counterpoint to her frenetic energy. "I will handle everything for the ceremony. The flowers, the music, even a photographer. The cruise director owes me a favor; she can find something suitable for you to wear."

"But my daughter, I have to…"

"Yes, of course. Go, tell Kelly and your friends. They should be the first to know." He guided her toward the door, his hand warm against the small of her back. "I'll send someone to find them if you can't. But everything else? Leave it to me."

Tessa nodded, but her fingers were already twisting her necklace, her foot tapping against the carpet. "Rings. We need rings. And I should call my financial advisor. And—"

"We sail with a jeweler aboard," Manny reminded her, amusement warming his voice. "One more thing to cross off your list."

He opened the door but held her there a moment longer, cupping her face in his hands. His expression shifted, becoming serious, almost reverent.

"Tessa," he said, his voice dropping to a near whisper. "I need you to know something before you go."

Her racing thoughts paused as she met his gaze.

"I love you." The words emerged unambiguous. "It feels impossible after so short a time, but I know it as surely as I know the stars or the tides. I have lived a solitary life, married to the sea, until now. But I want to share whatever years I have left with you, at sea, on land, wherever we find ourselves."

Tears sprang to Tessa's eyes, unexpected and overwhelming. All her frantic energy dissolved into something deeper, more certain.

"I love you too," she whispered back, the truth of it resonating through her. "God help me, I do."

He kissed her then, gently, sweetly, before pulling away. "Six o'clock," he reminded her. "Don't be late."

"I won't," she promised, and with one last look at his beloved face, she hurried down the corridor.

As she rushed toward the pool where she'd left Julia and Seren, her mind raced with logistics and doubts and impossible excitement. Sixty-two years of careful planning, and now she was getting married to a ship captain she'd known for eleven days, in less than four hours.

It was madness. Complete, utter madness.

And yet, beneath the panic and practical concerns, a surprising sense of rightness had settled in her chest. For the first time in decades, perhaps in her entire life, she was following her heart instead of her head. Jumping without knowing exactly where she would land.

The realization made her laugh out loud as she rushed through the ship, drawing curious glances from passing guests. Tessa Monroe, cautious, pragmatic, always-prepared Tessa, was leaping into the unknown.

And it felt glorious.

Chapter 22

Tessa moved swiftly across the deck, her sandals slapping noisily against the polished floorboards. Her mind buzzed with urgency, overwhelmed by Manny's unexpected proposal. But she pushed her thoughts aside when she spotted her friends: Seren, Julia, Liam, and Kelly, laughing around a table near the pool, a bottle of champagne chilling in an ice bucket beside them.

The sunlight dappled the scene with warmth, and Kelly waved energetically, calling for Tessa to join their impromptu celebration. "Mom! Over here! You won't believe it!"

Her confusion gave way to curiosity. Had Manny already told them? But how could they know?

As she approached, Kelly poured a glass of bubbly and handed it to her, her grin infectious and bright. Before Tessa could question them, her daughter placed the flute in her hand, the champagne fizzing prettily.

"Wait," Tessa began, her confusion evident but mingling with trepidation. "What's going on?"

Kelly glanced toward Julia with a conspiratorial gleam. Julia straightened, her smile wide and eyes sparkling with triumph. "I heard from my publisher this morning," she announced, joy threading through her voice. "They're going to publish my first book."

A cheer erupted, loud and spontaneous, as congratulations flowed amongst the group. Tessa found herself swept into the moment, her impending news temporarily eclipsed by Julia's achievement.

Julia gestured animatedly as she shared more, her face alight with excitement. "It's fiction, technically," she admitted, leaning toward Seren and Tessa, as if spilling secrets. "But it's inspired by all of us. Our lives. Gay husbands, cheating husbands, dying husbands, and us, strong women surviving it all."

Seren's eyes narrowed with mock suspicion. "Did you divulge anything too juicy, Jules?"

Julia laughed. "Oh, I embellished a little. That's what fiction is for, right?"

Tessa's mind tugged her back to her own urgent revelation, pressing her to speak. But Kelly, not skipping a beat, interrupted. "Wait, I've got news too," she said, her grin broadening as she exchanged a glance with Liam, who nodded.

Kelly took a deep breath, feigning suspense. "Liam managed to get Nate Berkus to design his New York condo!"

Gasps and laughter circled the table, the women expressing their amazement. Seren clapped her hands, half-jokingly demanding details.

Kelly shook her head, laughing at the playful disbelief. "But that's not the real news."

With anticipation crackling in the air, Kelly, almost conspiratorial, leaned in. "Liam's joining my firm. He's moving to San Francisco as soon as he can sell that condo."

Another round of cheers and clinks of champagne flutes sounded as congratulations and excitement filled the terrace. Tessa watched Liam, a grin on his face, accepting their applause with modesty.

For a moment, everything else faded: the warm sun, the vibrant sky, the distant hum of the ship, and all Tessa felt was joy for her daughter, for her friends. A sense of community wrapped around her like a beloved, well-worn sweater, comforting and precious.

And then Kelly, still beaming, turned to her, her voice cutting through the camaraderie. "Mum, you were about to say something?"

* * *

"I'm getting married," Tessa announced without preamble.

The clinking of glasses ceased. All conversation died mid-sentence. Four pairs of eyes fixed on her with varying degrees of shock.

"What?" Kelly burst out, her champagne sloshing over the rim of her glass.

"I'm getting married," Tessa repeated, her voice steadier this time. "Today. At six o'clock. To Manny." A smile broke across her face as the reality of her own words hit her. "He's been assigned to captain the Celestia: it's their newest ship. A hundred and eighty-seven-day world cruise leaving in two weeks. And I'm going with him."

The silence that followed felt electric. Julia's mouth opened and closed without producing sound. Seren's eyebrows had disappeared beneath her bangs.

"You're joking," Kelly finally managed, setting her glass down with a sharp click.

"I'm not." Tessa pulled out a chair and sat, her legs suddenly unsteady. "I know how it sounds. Believe me, I do. If one of you told me this, I'd think you'd lost your mind."

"Today?" Julia found her voice. "As in, four hours from now today?"

"Less than four, actually." Tessa glanced at her watch and felt a flutter of panic. "The Staff Captain is performing the ceremony in the ship's chapel."

"Wait, wait, wait." Kelly held up her hands. "You've known him for what… eleven days? And you're marrying him? Mom, that's…"

"Crazy? Impulsive? Completely out of character?" Tessa finished for her. "Yes. All of that. But it feels right." She leaned forward, trying to make them understand. "He's been offered this incredible opportunity, captaining a brand-new ship on its maiden voyage around the world. Thirty-two countries. Six continents."

"And you're what… dropping everything to sail off with him?" Kelly's voice had taken on a sharp edge.

"Yes." The simplicity of her answer seemed to hang in the air. "I've spent my entire life being practical, predictable, and responsible. I built a career, raised you, did everything by the book. And now there's this man, this wonderful, passionate man, who wants me by his side as he travels the world."

"But marriage?" Seren asked gently. "Couldn't you just… date long-distance for a while?"

Tessa shook her head. "Company policy. No unmarried partners living aboard, especially in the captain's quarters."

"So this is about… logistics?" Julia frowned.

"No." Tessa reached across the table, taking both Julia's and Seren's hands. "It's about love. He told me he loves me, and I love him. I didn't plan it, didn't expect it, but there it is."

Kelly's expression softened slightly. "You really love him?"

"I do," Tessa said, meeting her daughter's gaze. "More than I thought possible after your father."

The tension around the table eased, almost imperceptibly at first, then more noticeably as Liam broke into a wide grin.

"Well, I think it's fantastic," he declared, raising his glass. "To unexpected love!"

Seren's face transformed, caution giving way to excitement. "My God, Tess. You're really doing this!" She clapped her hands together. "A wedding! Tonight!"

"Which reminds me," Tessa said, nervousness creeping into her voice. "Will you help me get ready? I have nothing to wear; my hair is a mess, everything's already in my suitcase for disembarkation."

"Are you kidding?" Julia exclaimed, already on her feet. "Of course we'll help!"

Suddenly, all five of them were talking at once, plans forming and dissolving as quickly as they were proposed.

"The ship's boutique," Seren began.

"… might have something white…"

"… or cream, cream would be lovely with your coloring."

"I need to do something with my hair," Tessa fretted, running fingers through her chlorine-dampened bob.

"Your suite, Mom," Kelly declared authoritatively. "It's the largest. Aunt Seren, will you see what they have in the boutique? Aunt Julia, call the salon and insist they fit Mom in, after all, she's marrying the captain."

They scattered across the deck, purpose driving their movements, leaving half-full champagne glasses behind. As Tessa hurried alongside her daughter, she felt a wild, unfamiliar joy bubbling up inside her.

In less than four hours, she would be Mrs. Captain Delgado, sailing off on the adventure of a lifetime.

* * *

Tessa's stateroom had transformed into a bridal chamber within the hour. Flower arrangements materialized alongside trays of canapés, and the bed disappeared beneath garment bags and beauty products. The phone rang incessantly, first the cruise director confirming details, then the chef inquiring about menu preferences.

"Everything's under control," the cruise director assured Tessa, her voice brimming with efficiency. "We've arranged a champagne reception in the atrium immediately following the ceremony. How many guests would you like at the celebration dinner?"

Tessa felt momentarily overwhelmed. "Just our small group: my daughter, my two closest friends, and Liam. Five total, plus Manny and me."

"Perfect. We'll make it intimate and special."

The door burst open as Seren swept in, arms laden with garment bags, her bohemian skirts swishing dramatically around her ankles. "The boutique manager nearly fainted when I told her why I needed these," she announced, carefully laying three dresses across the sofa. "Apparently, the captain getting married on board is quite the event."

Tessa barely had time to examine the options before Julia arrived, ushering in a flustered-looking stylist and makeup artist. "They've rescheduled two appointments to fit you in," Julia explained proudly. "Once they heard you were the captain's bride-to-be..."

A gentle knock interrupted them. Kelly opened the door to reveal a waiter bearing an elaborate tray of hors d'oeuvres and a bottle of Dom Pérignon. "Compliments of Mr. McDougal," the waiter explained with a bow.

"Liam," Tessa murmured, genuinely touched by his thoughtfulness.

While Tessa showered, the room buzzed with activity. The stylist set up her tools, the makeup artist arranged her palette, and Kelly fielded calls from the ship's staff, who seemed determined to make this impromptu wedding as grand as any that had been planned for months.

Julia and Seren eventually retreated to their own cabins to dress, promising to return within the hour. Kelly stayed, watching her mother's transformation with a mixture of wonder and something that looked almost like wistfulness.

By five-thirty, Tessa stood before the mirror, barely recognizing herself. The cream-colored gown Seren had selected cascaded from her shoulders in a waterfall of silk and delicate crystals that caught the light with every breath she took. The sweetheart neckline revealed just enough collarbone to be elegant without being overly exposed, while the fitted bodice gave way to a flowing skirt that moved like water around her.

Her silver-gray hair had been styled into soft, romantic waves, with tiny diamond pins catching the light. The makeup artist performed miracles, highlighting her cheekbones and brightening her eyes without masking the features that made her uniquely Tessa. Around her neck hung a simple diamond pendant, her "something borrowed" from Julia.

"Mom," Kelly breathed, her eyes glistening. "You look…"

The door opened as Seren and Julia returned, both stopping short at the sight of Tessa.

Seren had chosen a flowing gown in deep teal that complemented her bohemian spirit while elevating it to evening elegance. Intricate silver embroidery adorned the bodice, and her wild hair had been tamed into an artful updo adorned with tiny silver flowers.

Julia wore a sophisticated column dress in midnight blue that skimmed her curves perfectly. A single strand of pearls circled her neck, and her chestnut hair fell in soft waves around her face, the silver streaks catching the light like threads of moonlight.

Kelly had changed into a sleek emerald dress that highlighted her tall, elegant figure and complemented her blonde waves, which she'd swept to one side with a jeweled clip.

"We clean up rather well, don't we?" Seren said with a delighted laugh, twirling to show off her dress.

Julia picked up the bottle of champagne Liam had sent and expertly poured four flutes. "One last toast," she said, passing the glasses around. When everyone had their drink, she raised hers high.

"To Tessa," Julia began, her voice rich with emotion. "Who taught us all how to be strong through the hardest moments of our lives. Who built a remarkable career while raising an extraordinary daughter." She paused, catching Kelly's eye with a warm smile. "Who always did the sensible thing, the right thing, the responsible thing, until today."

They all laughed softly, the tension of the earlier confrontation completely dissolved.

"Today," Julia continued, raising her glass higher, "you're teaching us another lesson entirely: that it's never too late to follow your heart. That love can find us when we least expect it. And that sometimes, the most beautiful adventures begin with a leap of faith."

"To leaps of faith," Seren added, her eyes sparkling.

"To new beginnings," Kelly said, her voice steady now, full of genuine happiness for her mother.

"To all of you," Tessa whispered, emotion threatening to undo the makeup artist's careful work. "For supporting me through every decision I've ever made, even the wildly impulsive ones."

They clinked glasses, the crystal ringing clear and bright, like a perfect note of music.

A soft knock at the door announced it was time. The ship's chapel was waiting, and so was Manny.

Tessa took one last look in the mirror, barely recognizing the radiant woman staring back at her. Gone was the practical attorney, the responsible mother, the predictable friend. In her place stood a bride, luminous with joy, trembling with anticipation, ready for adventure.

The four women stepped into the corridor, arms linked, headed toward the chapel where everything would change.

Chapter 23

The cruise director, a petite woman with an efficient manner and dazzling smile, glided through the ship's corridors with practiced ease, guiding the four elegantly dressed women toward the ship's chapel. The gentle hum of the engines beneath their feet mingled with the distant sounds of laughter and music as other passengers enjoyed their last evening aboard.

"Here we are, ladies," she announced as they reached a set of double doors inlaid with polished wood and stained glass. Julia and Seren squeezed Tessa's hands before slipping inside, leaving mother and daughter alone in the corridor.

Kelly turned to face her mother, her eyes searching Tessa's face. The hallway light caught the emerald of her dress, casting a subtle green glow between them.

"Mom," she said softly, taking both of Tessa's hands in hers. "Are you absolutely certain about this? It's so sudden, and once we go back home."

"I'm not going back home," Tessa said, her voice steady despite the butterflies in her stomach. "At least not yet. I'm going around the world with a man who makes me feel alive again."

Kelly's expression softened. "You really love him, don't you?"

"I do," Tessa whispered, surprised at how natural those two words felt. "This wasn't planned, Kelly, but it feels right in a way nothing has in years."

Kelly nodded, blinking back unexpected tears. "Then… let's get you married."

The chapel door swung open to reveal a space transformed. What had been a simple, elegant room for quiet reflection now bloomed with life. White and cream roses cascaded from pedestals along the aisle, their scent perfuming the air with sweetness. Candles flickered in hurricane lamps, casting a golden glow across the polished wood and glimmering brass fixtures. The stained-glass windows that lined the walls caught the setting Mediterranean sun, throwing jewel-toned patterns across the small gathering.

Liam stood near the front row beside Julia and Seren, handsome in a tailored navy suit. He gave Kelly a subtle wink as she took her place with the others.

At the front of the chapel, beneath an arch woven with more roses and trailing greenery, stood Manny. His captain's uniform gleamed white against the candlelight, gold braid catching the light as he shifted nervously from one foot to the other. When he looked up and saw Tessa, his restless movement stilled completely.

With the first notes of music, a string quartet playing softly from a corner, Tessa glided down the short aisle.

Manny's face transformed as Tessa approached, wonder and devotion replacing his earlier nervousness. His eyes never left hers as she moved toward him, step by measured step.

The Staff Captain, now newly promoted to full Captain of the Aurelia, waited at the center with an ancient leather-bound book. His voice carried clearly through the intimate space as he welcomed the small gathering.

"We are gathered here today, in accordance with maritime tradition, to join these two souls together on the vast ocean that has brought them to each other."

The ceremony unfolded with simple elegance, vows exchanged in voices that grew stronger with each word, rings produced from Manny's pocket (somehow, impossibly, he had found a pair of matching bands), and the traditional nautical blessing invoking calm seas and fair winds for their journey together.

"By the authority vested in me as Captain of this vessel, in international waters under maritime law, I now pronounce you husband and wife," the new Captain declared. "Captain Delgado, you may kiss your bride."

Manny cupped Tessa's face with gentle hands and kissed her with a tenderness that spoke volumes. The small chapel erupted in cheers and applause, led by Seren's enthusiastic whoops and Julia's more dignified but equally joyful clapping.

* * *

Crystalline chandeliers cast a warm glow over the small gathering in the ship's elegant Orion Lounge, transformed for the evening into an intimate reception venue. White roses and orchids adorned every table, their delicate fragrance mingling with the scents of fine cuisine being prepared in the galley. Floor-to-ceiling windows revealed the darkening Mediterranean sky, stars beginning to twinkle like distant promises above the inky sea.

Tessa and Manny stood near the entrance, hands clasped together, greeting their guests with radiant smiles. The newlyweds seemed to glow from within, their happiness creating an almost tangible aura around them.

"This is perfect," Tessa whispered to her husband, the word 'husband' still feeling wonderfully foreign on her tongue. "Small, intimate, just our closest friends."

Manny squeezed her hand. "And soon, the entire world will be explored together."

The ship's photographer circulated discreetly among the guests, capturing candid moments, Julia and Seren laughing together, Kelly deep in conversation with Liam, the Staff Captain sharing a story with the Chief Security Officer. Each flash preserved a memory of this unexpected celebration born of spontaneous love.

"Ladies and gentlemen," announced Sophie, the Cruise Director, her voice was melodious and practiced. "Please take your seats. Dinner is about to be served."

The small party settled around a single elegantly set table. Crystal glasses caught the light, fine china gleamed, and silver cutlery winked against crisp white linens. Manny sat Tessa with a flourish before taking his place beside her, his eyes never straying far from his bride's face.

"The Executive Chef has prepared something special for our celebration tonight," Sophie explained as white-gloved servers appeared with the first course. "A seven-course tasting menu inspired by Captain Delgado's Mediterranean heritage and the journey our newlyweds are about to embark upon."

Delicate amuse-bouches arrived first, miniature works of culinary art on porcelain spoons. Then came a velvety lobster bisque, followed by handmade ravioli filled with truffle and ricotta. Perfectly paired wines accompanied each course, the champagne flutes continuously refreshed with golden bubbles.

Between the fish course and the palate cleanser, Sophie tapped her glass gently. "It's time for toasts to the happy couple," she announced, turning to the Staff Captain with an elegant gesture.

The Staff Captain rose, his glass held high. "To Captain Manny Delgado, my friend and mentor," he began, his voice carrying across the intimate space. "You've navigated stormy seas and calm waters with equal skill. Now you've charted a new course, one shared with this remarkable woman. May your marriage be like the finest ship: strong enough to weather any storm yet always pointed toward new horizons. To Captain and Mrs. Delgado!"

"To Captain and Mrs. Delgado," echoed the guests, glasses raised.

Seren stood next, her bohemian dress shimmering in the candlelight. She raised her glass, her eyes twinkling with mischief and deep affection.

"To my dearest friend Tessa, who has finally, gloriously lost her mind," she declared, drawing laughter from around the table. "After decades of being the voice of reason, the sensible one, the planner, you've thrown caution to the Mediterranean winds and followed your heart. And what a beautiful direction it's taking you!" She turned to Manny, her expression softening. "Captain, you've found yourself a treasure beyond price. Take care of her, adventure with her, and know that if you don't," she winked dramatically, "you'll have to answer to me and Julia. To love, spontaneity, and second chances!"

As the laughter and applause subsided, Kelly rose somewhat tentatively, her champagne flute catching the light. Her eyes, like her mother's, shimmered with emotion.

"Mom," she began, her voice steady despite the emotion clearly visible on her face. "All my life, you've shown me what strength looks like. You've demonstrated the power of resilience, of grace under pressure, of putting one foot in front of the other even when the path seemed impossible." She paused, gathering herself. "But today, you've taught me something new, that it's never too late to rewrite your story. That love can arrive unexpectedly and change everything."

She turned to Manny, her expression warming. "Captain Delgado, I entrust you with my mother's heart. It's the most precious thing I know. Cherish it, as we all do." Kelly raised her glass higher. "To my mother and her captain, may your journey together be the greatest adventure of all!"

The evening continued with dessert, a masterpiece of chocolate and gold leaf, and dancing, as the ship's pianist played softly in the corner. Eventually, the small party began to disperse, with warm embraces and promises to meet for breakfast before disembarkation.

Hand in hand, Manny and Tessa made their way through the ship's corridors toward the captain's quarters. Every crew member they passed offered congratulations, a nod, a smile, or a quiet "Felicitations, Captain and Mrs. Delgado."

When they reached the door to his, now their, quarters, Manny swept Tessa into his arms with surprising strength, eliciting a delighted laugh from his new bride.

"I believe this is traditional," he murmured, kissing her softly as he carried her across the threshold.

Inside, the spacious quarters had been transformed. Rose petals formed a path across the floor, and dozens of candles bathed the room in golden light. A bottle of champagne was chilled beside the bed, and through the large windows, the stars seemed to have aligned just for them.

Manny set Tessa gently on her feet but kept his arms around her. "Are you happy, my love?" he asked, searching her face.

"Happier than I ever imagined possible," she answered honestly, her hands resting against his chest where she could feel his heart beating. "It's like I've been sleepwalking through life, and suddenly, I'm awake."

"I have captained ships for twenty-seven years," Manny said, his accent thickening with emotion. "I have sailed every sea, weathered every storm. But nothing… nothing has felt like this. Like finding home in another person."

Tessa reached up to touch his face, tracing the lines at the corners of his eyes, the distinguished silver of his beard. "So, what happens now, Captain Delgado?"

Manny smiled, the expression transforming his entire face. "Now, Mrs. Delgado, we begin our greatest voyage. Together."

As their lips met, the Aurelia continued its journey through the night, carrying them toward tomorrow and all the tomorrows that would follow, a world of possibilities stretching before them like an endless sea.

* * *

Dawn broke over the Mediterranean, painting the sky in shades of rose and gold as the Aurelia glided into Barcelona's harbor. The port bustled with activity, taxis lining up, luggage handlers preparing for the day's turnover, and the next wave of excited passengers gathering on the pier. For most, this was simply the beginning or end of a vacation, but for six people sharing breakfast in the ship's Aurum Restaurant, it marked a far more significant transition.

"I still can't believe you pulled off a wedding in three hours," Kelly said, spreading jam on a croissant while shaking her head in amazement. She'd already dressed for travel in tailored pants and a light cashmere sweater, her phone occasionally buzzing with messages she glanced at but didn't answer.

"The crew was extraordinary," Tessa replied, her fingers unconsciously finding Manny's beneath the table. She looked different this morning, her face glowing with happiness, her posture more relaxed than her friends had seen in decades.

Manny, still in his captain's uniform, nodded appreciatively. "They enjoy a break from routine. A wedding is always special on board."

"So, what happens next for everyone?" Julia asked, stirring her coffee thoughtfully. "We all seem to be heading in different directions."

"Kelly and I have the same flight to New York," Seren said, helping herself to another slice of melon from the fruit platter. "Then she continues to San Francisco, and I'll spend a night in the city before heading home."

Kelly nodded. "I can't wait to get back to Briana. We're meeting with a wedding planner next week." She turned to her mother. "I still can't believe you beat me to the altar, Mom."

Laughter rippled around the table as Tessa blushed prettily.

"And you, Julia?" Manny asked.

"Back to the Eastern Shore," Julia answered. "My publisher wants to discuss marketing plans for the book. There's talk of a small tour in the fall… nothing extensive, just a few cities."

"You'll be brilliant," Seren assured her, reaching over to squeeze her friend's hand. "First-time author at sixty-two, it's inspiring."

"What about your travel agency?" Tessa asked Seren. "Has the sale gone through?"

Seren nodded, her bohemian earrings catching the morning light. "The final paperwork should be ready when I get back. It's bittersweet, but it's time." A mischievous smile played across her lips. "Besides, I have other plans brewing. That olive grove in Capri hasn't left my mind."

"The one with Matteo?" Julia raised an eyebrow knowingly.

"Perhaps," Seren replied with a wink. "I've always wanted a retreat center in Italy. The universe seems to be pointing me in that direction."

Liam, who had been relatively quiet, set down his coffee cup. "I'll be back in New York tonight. The real estate agent is already lining up showings for my condo." He glanced at Kelly with a grateful smile. "Then it's off to San Francisco to start fresh."

"Vertex Ventures won't know what hit them," Kelly said confidently. "Briana's already found an apartment near us, temporarily, until you find your own place."

Manny turned to Tessa, his eyes crinkling warmly at the corners. "And we have our own journey to begin. The car will take us to the airport in an hour." His Italian accent thickened with excitement. "Trieste awaits, where the Celestia is completing her final sea trials."

"I still can't believe I'm going to live on a cruise ship," Tessa said, shaking her head in wonder.

"Not just any ship," Manny corrected proudly. "The newest, most advanced vessel in the fleet. And not just live on it, travel the world on it."

"One hundred and eighty-seven days," Tessa mused, a mixture of excitement and disbelief coloring her voice. "Thirty-two countries. I plan to fill my passport with stamps."

The conversation paused as a crew member discreetly approached Manny, murmuring something about disembarkation procedures. He nodded, then turned apologetically to the table.

"I must attend to some final duties before we leave. Perhaps twenty minutes." He kissed Tessa's hand before standing. "I'll meet you in the suite, cara mia."

After Manny departed, Kelly leaned toward her mother. "Are you nervous at all? This is such a massive change."

Tessa considered the question seriously. "Strangely, no. For the first time in my life, I'm not overthinking everything. I'm just… following my heart." She laughed softly. "And if that heart leads me on a ship around the world with a handsome Italian captain, who am I to argue?"

Their laughter mingled with the morning sunlight streaming through the windows, warming the space between them.

As breakfast concluded, the inevitable moment of parting approached. They gathered in the atrium, surrounded by the organized chaos of disembarkation. Other passengers streamed past, but for these few minutes, they created their own island of stillness.

"Call me as soon as you can," Kelly told her mother, embracing her tightly. "And I expect both of you at my wedding."

"We wouldn't miss it," Tessa promised, holding her daughter close.

Julia and Seren took turns hugging Tessa, their eyes bright with unshed tears and genuine happiness.

"You've inspired me," Julia whispered. "Taking risks, following joy, it's never too late."

"Send pictures from everywhere," Seren demanded. "Every port, every sunset."

Manny returned just in time for the final goodbyes, embracing each of them warmly. "You must all visit us on the Celestia," he insisted. "Anywhere in the world… just name the port."

With final waves and promises to stay connected, Julia, Seren, Kelly, and Liam joined the stream of departing passengers, disappearing down the gangway into the bright Barcelona morning.

Manny slipped his arm around Tessa's waist as they watched their friends go. "Ready for our next adventure, Mrs. Delgado?"

Tessa turned to face her husband, her heart full. The Mediterranean sparkled beyond the ship's windows, the world vast and waiting. "More than ready, Captain. Lead the way."

Chapter 24

Catania, Sicily

Full-Day Shore Excursion: The Spirit of Sicily—Mount Etna, Taormina & Sicilian Flavors.

Duration: 8 hours (full day)

Activity Level: Moderate (walking on uneven terrain)

Transportation: Air-conditioned minibus or coach with local guide.

Overview

Experience the drama, beauty, and soul of Sicily on this full-day exploration from Catania. Journey from the sea to the slopes of Mount Etna, Europe's highest active volcano… then unwind in the hilltop town of Taormina, where ancient ruins meet chic boutiques and sweeping Ionian views. Along the way, savor local wines and traditional Sicilian specialties for a day rich in culture, scenery, and flavor.

Highlights

- Walk on the lower slopes of Mount Etna, surrounded by ancient lava fields and lunar landscapes.

- Visit a local winery for a tasting of Etna DOC wines paired with artisanal cheeses and olive oil.

- Stroll the charming streets of Taormina, home to the spectacular Greek Theatre and views of Mount Etna and the Bay of Naxos.

- Explore Corso Umberto, lined with elegant shops, cafés, and gelaterias.

- Enjoy a scenic coastal drive back to Catania with commentary on Sicilian history and daily life.

* * *

Capri, Italy

Full-Day Shore Excursion: The Essence of Capri—Island Beauty, Local Flavors & Hidden Corners.

Port: Marina Grande, Capri (via tender from Naples, Sorrento, or Amalfi)

Duration: 8 hours (full day)

Activity Level: Moderate (walking on inclines and uneven surfaces)

Transportation: Private minibus, funicular, and optional boat tour.

Overview

Discover why Capri has enchanted artists, poets, and travelers for centuries. This full-day exploration reveals both sides of the island: glamorous Capri Town and the quieter, authentic Anacapri, along with breathtaking sea views, local cuisine, and hidden gardens. From lemon-scented lanes to panoramic terraces and artisan workshops, experience the island's soul beyond the postcard-perfect scenes.

Highlights

- Explore the village of Anacapri, known for its tranquil charm, artisan crafts, and sweeping vistas.

- Visit Villa San Michele or the Monte Solaro chairlift for unforgettable island views.

- Stroll through Capri Town and the famous Piazzetta, the island's elegant social hub.

- Wander the Gardens of Augustus overlooking the Faraglioni rock formations.

- Enjoy a leisurely Mediterranean lunch featuring local specialties and island-grown olive oil.

- Optional boat tour around the island, or a visit to the Blue Grotto (weather permitting).

It is important to note that the olive grove visited in Calmer Waters was fictionalized. However, it is possible to organize an excursion to an olive grove in Capri. I highly recommend working with a travel advisor, as olive grove tours are not offered daily and are often scheduled seasonally or by private arrangement.

Olive Grove and Olive Oil Experiences on Capri

Giardino di Capri—Cheese, Wine & Olive Oil Tasting

Located in Anacapri, this private experience includes a tasting of several varieties of extra virgin olive oil, paired with local cheeses and wines. Guests learn about olive cultivation and oil production while enjoying the relaxed setting of a family-run villa. Advance booking is required.

Guided Cheese, Wine & EVOO Tasting Experience

This two-hour tasting combines olive oil, cheese, and wine in a rustic garden setting in Anacapri. It's a lovely way to learn about the flavors and traditions of the island while sampling locally produced olive oils.

1. **L'Oro di Capri Olive Grove Initiative**

This local organization is dedicated to preserving Capri's historic olive groves. They occasionally host guided visits, workshops, and special events where visitors can walk among the trees and learn about traditional harvesting and pressing methods. These events are seasonal and usually take place during the olive harvest or local heritage celebrations.

* * *

Rome, Italy

Full-Day Shore Excursion: Eternal Rome—Ancient Wonders & Timeless Splendor.

Port: Civitavecchia (Rome)

Duration: 9–10 hours (full day)

Activity Level: Moderate to Active (extended walking and standing)

Transportation: Air-conditioned coach or private minivan with professional guide.

Overview

Step into the pages of history with this full-day journey from the Port of Civitavecchia to Rome, the Eternal City. From the grandeur of the Colosseum and Roman Forum to the artistic treasures of the Vatican, experience the landmarks that shaped Western civilization. Between iconic sights, enjoy authentic Roman cuisine and glimpses of daily life that make Rome unforgettable.

Highlights

- Walk inside the legendary Colosseum, Rome's most famous monument.

- Discover the Roman Forum and Palatine Hill, the heart of the ancient empire.

- Marvel at the Vatican Museums, Sistine Chapel, and St. Peter's Basilica.

- Savor a traditional Roman lunch featuring local pasta and wine.

- Enjoy a panoramic drive through the city, passing Piazza Venezia, the Pantheon, and the Trevi Fountain.

- Capture unforgettable photos at St. Peter's Square and other world-renowned landmarks.

* * *

Porto Cervo

Full-Day Shore Excursion: The Emerald Coast—Glamour, Villages & Flavors of Northern Sardinia.

Port: Porto Cervo, Sardinia (Tender or docked anchorage)

Duration: 7–8 hours (full day)

Activity Level: Easy to Moderate

Transportation: Air-conditioned minibus or private coach with local guide.

Overview

Explore the Emerald Coast (Costa Smeralda)—Sardinia's dazzling shoreline of turquoise bays, chic resorts, and rustic charm. This full-day excursion reveals the dual spirit of northern Sardinia: the luxurious elegance of Porto Cervo and the authentic character of the island's hill villages. Enjoy scenic drives, artisan encounters, and a leisurely Sardinian lunch paired with local wines.

Highlights

- Visit the glamorous village of Porto Cervo, the heart of Costa Smeralda.

- Enjoy a scenic coastal drive with breathtaking views of granite cliffs and emerald waters.

- Explore the traditional mountain village of San Pantaleo, known for local crafts and bohemian charm.

- Savor a farm-to-table Sardinian lunch featuring island cheeses, cured meats, and Vermentino wine.

- Visit a local winery or olive estate to taste regional specialties.

- Free time for shopping, strolling, or relaxing at a seaside café.

* * *

Portofino, Italy

Full-Day Shore Excursion: Enchanting Ligurian Riviera—Portofino, Santa Margherita & the Charm of the Italian Coast

Port: Portofino (Tender or via Santa Margherita Ligure)

Duration: 7–8 hours (full day)

Activity Level: Easy to Moderate

Transportation: Private minibus, ferry, and walking tour with a local guide

Overview

Experience the allure of Italy's Riviera di Levante, where pastel villages, shimmering seas, and pine-clad hills create one of the Mediterranean's most romantic landscapes. From the seaside elegance of Santa Margherita Ligure to the picture-perfect harbor of Portofino, this full-day excursion reveals the best of Ligurian beauty, cuisine, and coastal charm.

Highlights

- Explore the exclusive harbor village of Portofino, jewel of the Italian Riviera.

- Stroll along the palm-lined promenade of Santa Margherita Ligure.

- Visit the Church of San Giorgio or climb to Castello Brown for panoramic views.

- Enjoy a Ligurian-style lunch featuring fresh seafood, pesto, and local wines.

- Optional boat cruise along the coast or visit to the serene Abbey of San Fruttuoso.

- Time for shopping, gelato, and leisurely exploration of seaside cafés.

* * *

Nice, France

Full-Day Shore Excursion: The French Riviera—Nice, Eze & the Glamour of the Côte d'Azur.

Port: Villefranche-sur-Mer or Monaco (for Nice)

Duration: 7–8 hours (full day)

Activity Level: Moderate (walking and some uphill streets)

Transportation: Air-conditioned minibus or coach with local guide.

Overview

Experience the heart of the French Riviera—where old-world charm meets Mediterranean elegance. This full-day excursion takes you through the coastal beauty and refined atmosphere of Nice, the perched medieval village of Èze, and the glamour of Monte Carlo or Cannes (depending on your sailing route). With its vivid colors, open-air markets, and coastal panoramas, this day captures the essence of the Côte d'Azur: chic, sunlit, and effortlessly stylish.

Highlights

- Discover Old Nice (Vieux Nice) with its narrow lanes, flower market, and pastel façades.

- Stroll along the iconic Promenade des Anglais, lined with Belle Époque architecture and sea views.

- Visit the hilltop village of Èze, known for its cobbled streets, perfumeries, and stunning vistas.

- Enjoy a French Riviera lunch featuring Provençal specialties and local rosé.

- Optional visit to Monaco and Monte Carlo or Cannes, depending on port location and interests.

- Experience the timeless elegance and Mediterranean lifestyle that define the Côte d'Azur.

* * *

Marseille (Livorno), France

Full-Day Shore Excursion: Marseille & Provence—History, Coastline & Local Flavors

Port: Marseille, France

Duration: 8 hours (full day)

Activity Level: Moderate (walking on cobbled streets and some hills)

Transportation: Air-conditioned minibus or coach with local guide

Overview

Discover the vibrant port city of Marseille, gateway to the Provence region, where Mediterranean culture, history, and cuisine intertwine. This full-day excursion combines Marseille's maritime charm with the scenic beauty of the nearby Provençal countryside. Explore ancient fortresses, colorful neighborhoods, and coastal panoramas, all while savoring the flavors and traditions that make Southern France so unique.

Highlights

- Explore Vieux-Port (Old Port), the historic heart of Marseille, and its bustling fish market.

- Visit Basilique Notre-Dame de la Garde, perched above the city with sweeping views of the Mediterranean.

- Stroll through the Le Panier district, the oldest neighborhood in Marseille, with narrow streets, artisan shops, and street art.

- Enjoy a Provençal lunch featuring local seafood, bouillabaisse, and regional wines.

- Optional scenic drive along the Calanques, limestone cliffs and turquoise coves between Marseille and Cassis.

- Experience the vibrant culture, history, and Mediterranean flair of Marseille and its surroundings.

* * *

Palma de Mallorca, Spain

Full-Day Shore Excursion: Palma de Mallorca—History, Coast, and Local Flavors.

Port: Palma de Mallorca, Spain

Duration: 7–8 hours (full day)

Activity Level: Moderate (walking on city streets and slight inclines)

Transportation: Air-conditioned minibus or coach with local guide.

Overview

Discover the charm and elegance of Palma de Mallorca, the island's capital, where medieval streets, stunning cathedrals, and Mediterranean vistas converge. This full-day excursion offers a mix of history, culture, and local flavors, from the imposing La Seu Cathedral and winding old town lanes to coastal viewpoints and artisan workshops. Enjoy regional cuisine, panoramic views, and a taste of Mallorca's unique heritage.

Highlights

- Explore Palma's Old Town, with its narrow streets, boutique shops, and historic squares.

- Visit La Seu Cathedral, a Gothic masterpiece overlooking the Bay of Palma.

- Discover the Royal Palace of La Almudaina, blending Islamic and European architectural influences.

- Enjoy a Mallorcan lunch featuring local specialties such as sobrassada, ensaimada, and freshly caught seafood.

- Optional scenic drive along the coast to Port de Sóller or the Mirador de Sa Foradada.

- Experience the vibrant culture, Mediterranean lifestyle, and historic charm of Mallorca.

* * *

Barcelona, Spain

In the storyline, the characters do not actually tour Barcelona; they head directly to the airport. However, there are a couple of ship-to-airport excursions that may be available depending upon the cruise line you sail with.

Panoramic Highlights of Barcelona with Airport Transfer

Duration: ~4–5 hours. Perfect for: First-time visitors who want to see the city's icons without walking too much.

Overview

After disembarking, enjoy a comfortable coach tour through Barcelona's highlights—Montjuïc Hill for sweeping city views, Passeig de Gràcia to see Gaudí's masterpieces (*Casa Batlló*, *La Pedrera*), and a photo stop at the Sagrada Família. Continue along the waterfront before being dropped off directly at the airport.

Why it works: Scenic, relaxed, and efficient—no luggage handling or rushing.

Gaudí & Modernist Barcelona with Airport Transfer

Duration: ~5 hours. Perfect for: Art and architecture lovers.

Overview

Visit Park Güell, Gaudí's whimsical mosaic park, and enjoy a guided visit to the Sagrada Família (often with skip-the-line entry). You'll learn about Gaudí's life and vision, then transfer comfortably to the airport.

Why it works: Combines two iconic sites with seamless logistics.

Cava Country & Montserrat with Airport Drop-Off

Duration: ~6 hours (best for afternoon flights after 3:30 p.m.) Perfect for: Repeat visitors who want a relaxed countryside finale.

Overview

Travel to the Montserrat mountain monastery, known for its dramatic peaks and Black Madonna statue, then stop at a nearby Cava winery for a tasting and light tapas lunch before heading to the airport.

Why it works: Peaceful setting, minimal walking, and a memorable farewell to Spain.

Barcelona Market, Tapas & City Drive with Airport Transfer

Duration: ~4.5 hours. Perfect for: Foodies and culture seekers.

Overview

Visit La Boqueria Market with a local guide, sample small bites at a tapas bar, then enjoy a panoramic drive through the Gothic Quarter, Olympic Port, and Montjuïc before your airport drop-off.

Why it works: A taste of Barcelona's flavors without strenuous activity or tight timing.

Leisurely Morning in Park Güell & Montjuïc

Duration: ~4 hours. Perfect for: Travelers with earlier flights or who prefer a calm morning.

Overview

Walk gently through Park Güell, take photos from Montjuïc's lookout points, and enjoy coffee with a view before heading directly to the airport.

Why it works: Simple, scenic, and restorative, ideal for wrapping up your cruise vacation.

Author's Note

Thank you for reading Calmer Waters, the second book in the Navigating New Beginnings series. Please look for the final book in the series, Olive Skies, to be released soon.

The *Selene Voyages Aurelia*—the second vessel introduced in this series—is a fictional creation, inspired by a blend of real cruise lines and ships. I envisioned her as a compact, upscale vessel focused on exceptional cuisine, attentive service, and enrichment rather than large-scale entertainment. Instead of Broadway-style productions, guests aboard the *Aurelia* enjoy intimate musical performances, culinary demonstrations, and educational lectures. Within these imagined voyages, the ports of call themselves serve as the main attraction.

If this style of travel appeals to you, consider consulting a professional Travel Advisor, who can recommend a real-life voyage offering a similar ambiance and itinerary.

Several luxury and premium cruise lines offer itineraries comparable to the one depicted in Calmer Waters. A Travel Advisor can help you find the sailing that best suits your personal interests, comfort level, and budget.

My goal was to provide readers with an authentic sense of place in each Mediterranean port visited during the *Aurelia*'s voyage. The excursions, tours, and activities described are based on real itineraries, curated with women travelers (and Liam) in mind, specifically women in their sixties who are confident, curious, and active, apart from Kelly and her nut allergy, of course.

The sample itineraries are meant to inspire you. Each itinerary listed can be arranged through a reputable travel advisor.